WOLVES
and Other Love Stories

WOLVES

& Other Love Stories

IVAN BUNIN

*Russia's first Nobel Prize
winner in literature*

Translated from the Russian by Mark Scott

CAPRA PRESS / 1989

Cover design by Cyndi Brooks
Typography and book design by Jim Cook/Santa Barbara

LIBRARY OF CONGRESS CATALOGING-IN-PUBLICATION DATA
Bunin, Ivan Alekseevich, 1870-1953
    [Short stories. English. Selections]
    Wolves and other love stories of Ivan Bunin / translated from the
Russian by Mark C. Scott
        p.   cm.
    ISBN 0-88496-303-9: $9.95 (pbk.)
    1. Bunin, Ivan Alekseevich, 1870-1953—Translations, English.
I. Title.
PG3453.B9A613   1989
891.73'3—dc20   89-9994 CIP

Published by CAPRA PRESS
Post Office Box 2068
Santa Barbara, California 93120

Contents

Foreword

IVAN ALEXEYEVICH BUNIN (1870-1953) was the first Russian awarded the Nobel prize for literature (1933). His admirers—including Maxim Gorky—considered him a master stylist of the Russian language. Bunin's poems and short stories focus on timeless themes: the haunting power of sexual passion, the impermanence of love between men and women, the fusion of love and death, and the spiritual enigma of life.

Virulently hostile to Bolshevism, Bunin emigrated from Russia in 1919, never to return. He continued his literary career in France, where he died in poverty. During Bunin's lifetime, none of his writings were published in the USSR. However, Soviet editions of selected works appeared in the years immediately following his death.

Yet times do change. A "Bunin craze" seems to be afoot among Soviet youth. Surely, Ivan Bunin is the most unique dissident writer. His sensitive treatment of elusive, bittersweet love, of certain death—of the riddle of it all—has won him the love of the country he forsook.

MARK SCOTT
DECEMBER 1985

From the Author

I come from an old gentry family whose origins the *Heraldry of Gentry Families* describes as follows:

"The Bunins can be traced to Simeon Bunkovsky, a nobleman who came from Lithuania with his retinue in the fifteenth century to render military service to the Muscovite Grand Duke Vasily Vasilevich."

Our family has given Russia many prominent figures in the governmental arena—army commanders, members of the tsar's entourage, and those "of other ranks." In literature, Anna Bunina, whom Karamzin called the "Russian Sappho," is well-known, as is Vasily Zhukovsky, the natural son of Tula landowner Afanasy Ivanovich Bunin and the Turkish captive Salkha. Because of the circumstances of his birth, he was named Zhukovsky after his godfather. He was known more than anything else for being the founder of a new Russian literature. Its first genius, Pushkin, called Zhukovsky his teacher.

On my mother's side of the family, I belong to the Chubarovs, a gentry family, also an extremely old line. Family tradition has it that the Chubarovs were stripped of the title of prince under Peter the Great, who punished Prince Chubarov, a *strelets* colonel, for siding with Tsarevna Sofia.

All my ancestors had close ties to the Russian people and the land. The fathers and grandfathers of both my parents were landowners, with estates in central Russia, in that fertile area south of the steppes where the Muscovite tsars created outposts of settlers from various Russian regions to guard the State against the incursions of Southern Tartars. For this reason, it was a region which gave rise to a Russian language of great richness, a region from which almost all the greatest Russian writers have come, with Tolstoy in the forefront.

I was born on October 10, 1870, in Voronezh. I spent my childhood and early youth in the country, where at a young age I began writing and having my works published. Rather soon, even the critics began noticing me. Subsequently, my books achieved recognition. Three times, I received the highest award of the Russian Academy of Sciences—the Pushkin Prize. In 1909, the Academy selected me to be among its twelve Distinguished Members, who included Tolstoy. Still, I was more or less unknown for a long time, as I did not belong to any one school of literature. Besides that, I had little to do with the literati, spent much of my time in the country, and traveled extensively throughout Russia and abroad—Italy, Turkey, Greece, Palestine, Egypt, Algeria, Tunisia, and the tropics.

My popularity started with the publication of *The Village*. This was the beginning of a whole series of my works which sharply sketched the Russian soul, its light and dark—often tragic—roots. These "merciless" works of mine aroused the passionate, hostile reaction of Russian critics and intelligentsia who either did not know the Russian people or almost always idealized them for political reasons. During those years, I felt my literary powers grow every day. But then war broke out, then revolution.

I was not among those who had been caught off guard by

the Revolution, who had not anticipated its magnitude or brutality. Yet all the same, what it became in reality surpassed anything even I had expected. No one who did not actually see it can comprehend what the Russian Revolution quickly turned into. The spectacle was sheer terror for anyone who had not utterly lost sight of God. After Lenin seized power, hundreds of thousands of people fled Russia. Those who had the slightest chance of escaping did so. I abandoned Moscow on May 21, 1918, and lived in the south of Russia, in that region which passed back and forth between the "Whites" and the "Reds." Enduring untold sufferings of the spirit, I emigrated first to the Balkans, then to France. In France, I lived first in Paris, and in the summer of 1923 moved to the Coastal Alps, returning to Paris for only several months in the winter. I received the Nobel Prize in 1933.

As an émigré, I have written ten new books.

I. BUNIN
PARIS
OCTOBER 17, 1952

Wolves

THE DARKNESS OF A WARM August night. Dull stars barely visible, twinkling here and there in the cloudy sky. A soft road muffled by thick dust running through a field. Along the road a peasant wagon bounces as it carries two young passengers—the lady of a small estate and a young man, a Gymnasium student. The clouded summer lightning occasionally reveals a pair of work horses in the darkness; they have tangled manes, are in simple harnesses, and are running in tandem. The lightning also reveals the cap and shoulders of a peasant boy wearing a flapping shirt and sitting on the driver's seat. For an instant, the lightning illumines fields ahead now bare of farm workers, and flashes its light onto a distant, mournful grove.

In the village the night before, there had been noises, cries, the cowardly barking and yelping of dogs. While peasants were still eating dinner in their *izbas*, a wolf had with amazing boldness cut a sheep's throat in one farmyard and nearly carried it away. At the sound of barking dogs, peasants had jumped up in time and clubbed the sheep away from the wolf, beating the prey along its already dead, mutilated side. Now the lady is roaring with laughter, lighting wooden matches and throwing them into the darkness as she gaily shouts:

"I'm scared of wolves!"

The matches cast their flickering light onto the youth's excited, broad-cheeked, pretty face, which seems to sulk all the more. She has tightly tied a red shawl over her head, just like women do in Little Russia. The open throat of her red cotton dress exposes a round, firm neck. As the wagon bounces along the road, she lights matches and throws them into the darkness, as if not noticing that the student is hugging her and kissing first her neck, then her cheek, then searching for her lips. She shoves him aside with her elbow. Knowing that the peasant boy on the driver's seat can hear him, he exhorts her loudly:

"Blow out the matches! Smoking's not what I want!"

"In a minute, in a minute!" she cries, and again strikes a match, making it flare up. The lightning flashes and the darkness becomes even thicker—a warm blackness into which the wagon seems to be traveling backwards. Finally, she yields her lips to his prolonged kisses, when suddenly the wagon hits something, jolting them all. The peasant boy abruptly reins in the horses.

"Wolves!" he cries.

And a glowing fire far to the right strikes his eyes.

The wagon is standing across from that grove revealed by flashes of lightning. The grove has now turned black in the fire's glow. All of it is quivering unsteadily, just as the entire field in front of them is quivering in the gloomy red trembling of that fire being greedily borne into the sky. Despite the distance, the sky is blazing as shadows of smoke race into it. Burning as though it were a verst from the wagon, it blazes hotter, furiously hotter, more threatening, consuming the horizon ever higher and wider. It seems as if its heat is already reaching their faces, their hands.

The red mesh of someone's burning roof is visible even above the earth's blackness. And at the foot of the forest wall stand three great wolves—a scarlet gray. Their eyes smolder with a brilliant green, then red—watery and bright, like hot jam made from red currants. The horses snort loudly and rush to the left in a wild gallop across the pasture. The peasant boy leans back on the reins, yet the wagon—reeling, rumbling and rattling—hits the earth in leaps.

Somewhere not far from the edge of the ravine, the horses lunged even more violently. But she jumped up and managed to wrestle the reins from the confused boy. In one rapid motion, she flew onto the driver's seat, cutting her cheek against a sharp piece of iron. So for the rest of her life, a small scar remained at the corner of her lips. And whenever anyone would ask her what had caused it, she would smile with pleasure and say:

"Love affairs of long ago!" Then she would remember that distant summer, the dry days and dark nights of August, threshing on the threshing floor, stacks of fresh-smelling straw, and the unshaven student with whom she lay on those stacks in the evenings as the two of them watched the bright, momentary arcs of falling stars. "The wolves scared them, the horses bolted," she would say. "But I was a hot-blooded, desperate woman. I rushed to stop them . . ."

Those whom she had not yet loved said there was nothing sweeter than this scar, which resembled a thin, perpetual smile.

[1940]

Late at Night

WAS IT A DREAM, OR ONLY the late-night hour of some enigmatic life resembling a dream? It seemed to me that the sorrowful autumn moon had long, long since drifted above the earth, that the hour for resting from all lies and daily cares had at last come. All of Paris, down to its last pocket of poverty, seemed to have fallen asleep. I, too, slept for some time. Finally, a dream slowly left me, left as if it were an anxious, unhurried physician who had treated his patient and gone while the sick man was yet breathing deeply, and with open eyes smiling a bashful, joyous smile at life's return. As I awoke, I opened my eyes and saw I was in the peaceful, bright kingdom of the night.

I silently paced the carpet of my fifth-floor apartment to one of the windows. I looked at the room, large and filled with a faint twilight. Through the upper windowpane, the moon drenched me in its light. I gazed up into its face. Passing through the white lace curtain, the moonlight softened the twilight deep within the room. I couldn't see the moon from here, yet it cast its bright light on all four windows as if it were right next to them. Moonlight fell from the windows in pale-blue, silver-white arcs, each one enfolding the hazy shadow of a cross which softly crumbled as it stretched across the bright divans and armchairs. And she, the one I loved, was sitting in an armchair by the farthest window. In the whiteness, she looked like a little girl, white and lovely, wearied by all we had endured, all that had so often made us vicious and merciless enemies.

Why was she too not sleeping this night?

Trying not to look at her, I sat at the window by her side. Yes, it was late. The entire fifth-floor wall of the buildings across from us was dark. The windows were black, like blind eyes. I glanced below. The narrow, deep passageway of the street was also dark and empty. It was like this all over the city. Only the white, shining moon, tilting slightly, rolled on while standing still among the hazy, scudding clouds forlornly awake above the city. In all his brightness, the moon looked me straight in the face. Yet he was slightly waning, and for this reason was sad. Clouds, like smoke, drifted past him. Near him, they were bright and melted away. Farther on, they thickened and beyond the crest of rooftops passed by as a gloomy, heavy cloud bank.

I had not seen a moonlit night for such a long time! And so my thoughts returned once more to the distant, almost forgotten autumn nights of my childhood amid the hilly, sparse steppe lands of central Russia. There the moon had peered under the roof of my ancestral home, and there for the first time I had fallen in love with its gentle, pale face. My mind abandoned Paris, and for a split second all of Russia appeared before me. It was as if I were looking down onto vast lowlands. There was the sparkling, golden, deserted emptiness of the Baltic Sea. Over there were sullen lands of pine trees trailing off into the twilight to the east. Over there the scattered forests, marshes, and thickets. Down below, endless fields and plains stretched to the south. Railroad tracks slid for a hundred *versts* through the woods and faintly sparkled in the moonlight. Along the tracks, drowsy, multicolored little lights twinkled, each in turn leaving for my motherland. Gentle, rolling fields in front of me, and amid them—an old, gray manor house appearing decrepit, meek in the moonlight. Was this really the same moon that had once looked into my nursery, seen me then as a boy, and now grieved with me over my failed youth? He soothed me now in the bright domain of the night.

"Why aren't you sleeping?" a timid voice asked me.

And the fact that she was the first to turn to me after a long and stubborn silence painfully, yet sweetly, pierced my heart. I softly replied, "I don't know . . . And you?"

We were again silent for a long time. The moon had noticeably descended to the roof tops and was already looking deep into the room.

"Forgive me!" I said as I walked to her.

She didn't answer, just covered her eyes with both hands.

I held those hands and took them from her eyes. Tears were rolling down her cheeks. Her eyebrows arched and quivered like a child's. And I fell on my knees at her feet, pressed my face to her, sparing neither my tears nor hers.

"But are you really the one to blame?" she whispered in confusion. "Aren't I really to blame for everything?"

She smiled through her tears, a joyful, bitter smile.

And I told her that both of us were guilty because together we had broken the commandment of joy which should govern our lives. We again loved each other as only they can who suffer together, wander together, yet who together find rare, fleeting moments of truth. And only the pale, sorrowful moon saw our happiness . . .

[1899]

In the Autumn

SILENCE FELL FOR A MOMENT
on the living room. Taking advantage of the opportunity,
she stood up and glanced at me.

"Well, it's time," she said with a gentle sigh. My heart
quivered with the anticipation of some great joy, some great
mystery between us.

I hadn't left her side all evening. All evening, I had
detected a certain look in her eyes, a repressed luster, an
absentmindedness, and a barely noticeable tenderness that
was somehow new. Now, in the tone of her voice—the way
she regretfully told me it was time to go—there seemed to be
a hidden meaning, as if she knew I would be leaving with
her.

"Are you going too?" she asked hesitantly. "I mean,
you'll see me off, won't you?" she casually added. She was
having a difficult time playing this role, and smiled as she
glanced back at me.

With an easy, natural movement of the hand, she grabbed
the skirt of the black dress covering her slender, lithe body.
The shyness of a girl in love for the first time was there in
her smile, in the young, elegant face, the black eyes and
black hair, even—it seemed—in the thin string of pearls

around her neck and the brilliance of the diamonds in her earrings. The others were asking her to give their regards to her husband as they helped her on with her coat in the front hallway. I counted the seconds, fearing that someone would leave with us.

A strip of light momentarily fell onto the dark courtyard as the door opened, then gently closed. As I took her hand and carefully led her down the porch steps, I tried to restrain my nervous trembling while feeling an unusual lightness throughout my body.

"Can you see all right?" she asked, looking at the ground.

Once more, I could hear an encouraging friendliness in her voice.

Stepping through puddles and leaves, I led her in a roundabout way through the courtyard past bare acacias and the stinging scent of trees. Like riggings of sailing ships, they droned resoundingly, resiliently beneath the strong, damp wind of a November night in the South.

The carriage lantern shone through the grating of the gates. I glanced at her face. Without reply, she grasped the gate's iron bar with her small hand clad in a tight-fitting glove. She opened the gate halfway without my help, hurried through, and sat in the carriage. Just as quickly, I sat beside her . . .

II

We said nothing for a long time. Everything that had aroused our passions the past month was now said without a word. And we were silent only because saying it would have been too explicit, too unexpected. I pressed her hand to my lips and turned away in excitement, staring at the streets rushing toward us from the gloomy distance. I still feared her. When I asked her a question in a friendly manner, she only moved her lips in a weak smile, unable to answer—I knew that she too was afraid.

20

We could hear the sound of the Southern wind in the trees lining the boulevards. Flames of gas lamps occasionally appeared, flickering at street intersections. Signboards creaked above the doors of darkened shops. From time to time, a hunched figure and its swaying shadow would grow larger beneath the large, swinging lantern of a tavern. But the lantern would disappear behind us, and the street would again be empty. Only the damp wind would gently, unceasingly strike the faces of people walking here and there.

The carriage wheels spattered dirt in all directions. The dirt seemed interested in following the moving wheels. Now and then, I would glance at her lowered eyebrows, at the bowed profile beneath the hat. I felt her closeness to me, heard the faint aroma of her hair, was excited even by the smooth, soft sable around her neck . . .

Then we turned off onto a street—broad, empty, and long—which seemed as if it would never end. Rows of old Jewish shops and the marketplace passed by, then the pavement came to an abrupt halt. She shook from the jolt, and I instinctively embraced her. She glanced ahead, then turned to me. We looked into each other's eyes. Neither fear nor indecision remained in hers. I could sense a slight shyness in only her tense smile. And then not conscious of what they were doing, my lips swiftly clung tightly to hers . . .

III

In the darkness, we caught glimpses of the tall silhouettes of telegraph poles along the road. Even they finally vanished, going off somewhere to the side and disappearing. The sky, which had been black above the city yet had shunned the faintly lit streets, here blended into the earth. We were surrounded by a windy murkiness. I looked behind me. The city lights—sprinkled as if floating on a dark sea—had also disappeared. There was only a twinkling glow directly ahead of us. It was the old Moldavian inn on the highway—

lonely, faraway, as if at the edge of the earth. A strong wind flowed from that direction, swirling and hurriedly rustling through the dry cornstalks.

"Where are we going?" she asked, trying not to let her voice tremble. Yet her eyes were shining. Leaning toward her, I could see them in the darkness. They looked strange, yet happy.

The wind hastily rustled, raced, swirled amidst the corn, blowing straight into the horses' faces. Again, we turned off to the side, and the wind suddenly changed, became damper, cooler, and blew with greater tranquility.

I inhaled the wind. On this night, I wished that everything dark, obscure, and incomprehensible would be even more incomprehensible and daring. The night of bad weather which I thought had been so ordinary in the city was quite different here in the fields. There was now something great, something powerful in its wind and darkness. And then at last we could hear a certain steady, monotonous, majestic sound coming through the rustle of tall weeds.

"The sea?" she asked.

"The sea," I replied. "These already are the last dachas."

And in the pale darkness, a darkness now not so forbidding, the immense, gloomy silhouettes of poplars growing in dacha gardens rose up on our left, then led down to the sea. For a moment, the dull sound of the carriage wheels and the trampling of horses' hooves in the dirt reverberated distinctly against garden fences. Yet they were soon drowned out by the onrushing hum of trees, where the wind and sound of the sea were swirling. Several houses tightly boarded-up passed by. They appeared faintly white, seemingly dead. Then the poplars separated, and the passageway between them suddenly smelled of dampness, of that same wind which came flying to earth from immense watery expanses, and seemed to be their breath of freshness.

The horses stopped.

At that instant, we could hear it—the steady, majestic murmuring. We felt the enormous weight of the water in that murmur. We could even hear the chaotic humming of trees in gardens dozing restlessly. We hurriedly set off through leaves and puddles on a tall, tree-lined path leading to a cliff.

IV

Beneath the cliff, the sea droned in a threatening way, droned unlike all the other sounds of this uneasy, drowsy night. The sea lay far below, its immensity disappearing into the expanse. In the distance, crests of foam racing to earth turned white in the semi-darkness. Even the disorderly hum of old poplars from behind a garden fence had become frightening. The garden was like a dark island growing on a rocky shoreline. We could feel that the late autumn night was now ruling imperiously over this deserted place. The large old garden, the house boarded up for the winter, and the bare gazebos at the corners of the garden seemed alarming in their abandonment. Only the sea hummed steadily, victoriously, and—it seemed—all the more majestically, as if acknowledging its own strength.

The damp wind gathered at our feet as we stood at the edge of the cliff. For a long time, we could not get enough of its gentle freshness, a freshness which seemed to penetrate to the depths of my heart. Then, slipping on wet clay paths and the remnants of wooden steps, we descended to the surf, glittering with foam. Stepping onto the gravel, we jumped back from waves shattering against a rock. Black poplars towered and hummed. As if in reply, the sea playfully arched into ravenous, furious breakers. Steep waves, sounding like the crash of cannon fire, came flying toward us and spilled onto the shore. Then, like entire waterfalls of snowy foam, they turned and sparkled. The waves dug into sand and stone. Racing back, they took with them tangled seaweed or gravel which roared and gnashed in the wet clamor. The air was filled with a faint, cool dust. We could smell an uncontrolled freshness in the air. As the darkness paled, we could see water stretching into the distant expanse.

"And we're alone!" she said, closing her eyes.

V

We were alone. I kissed her lips, intoxicated by their moist tenderness. I kissed her eyes, which she offered me. I covered them with a smile, then kissed the face growing cold from the sea wind. And when she sat down on a rock, I was drained by my joy as I knelt before her.

"And tomorrow?" she asked from above.

I looked up into her face. Behind me, the sea raged with greed. Above us, the poplars soared and hummed . . .

"What about tomorrow?" I repeated, feeling my voice quaver from tears of invincible happiness. "What about tomorrow?"

She did not reply for a long time. Then she reached out to me, and I began slipping off her glove. Kissing both her hand and glove, I rejoiced in their faint, female aroma.

"Yes!" she said slowly. And in the starlight I studied her pale, happy face. "When I was a girl, I always dreamt of happiness. But everything has turned out to be so dull and ordinary. Right now, this night—possibly the only happy night in my life—seems unreal, criminal. Tomorrow, I'll be horrified when I think back on it. But now I don't care . . . I love you," she said tenderly, softly. She was deep in thought, talking as if to herself.

The bluish stars scattered overhead twinkled fleetingly between storm clouds. The sky had partially cleared, the poplars at the edge of the cliff were not as black, and the sea was gradually separating from the far horizon. Was she better than the others I have loved? I do not know. Yet that night she was without equal. When I kissed the dress on her

24

knees, she laughed quietly through her tears and held my head in her arms. I looked at her with ecstatic madness. And in the faint starlight, her pale, happy, weary face seemed deathless.

[1901]

In August

THE GIRL I LOVED WENT AWAY, the girl I never told I loved. And as I was only twenty-two at the time, it seemed I had no one else in the whole world. It was the end of August. A sultry calm lay over the Little Russian town where I was living. One Saturday, I left the barrel maker's shop after work. The streets were so empty that I didn't walk home, but wandered where my eyes led me beyond the city limits. I walked along the sidewalks past the closed Jewish stores, past the old stalls where merchants sold their wares. The church bells sounded vespers, and long shadows stretched from the houses. It was as hot as it usually is in Southern cities during late August, when everything is covered with dust, even gardens the sun has roasted throughout the summer. I was sad, indescribably sad, yet everything around me—the gardens, steppe, melon fields, even the air and thick sunshine—was dying from too much happiness.

A large beautiful Ukrainian woman stood by a pump on a dusty square. She was wearing a white, embroidered blouse and black skirt. Buckets were hanging tautly from her shoulders. On her bare feet, she was wearing shoes with iron taps. She somehow resembled the Venus de Milo, if you could image Venus suntanned, with gay eyes the color of coal, and that clear forehead which, it seems, is characteristic only of the women in Little Russia and Poland. Filling her buckets, she put the yoke on her shoulders and walked directly toward me. Standing straight despite the weight of the splashing water, she rocked her hips gently and tapped the iron soles of her shoes on the wooden sidewalk . . . And I remember how long I watched her walk into the distance! On my way to the Podol, I entered a street which led from the square to the foot of the mountain. I could see the immense, softly-shining valley of river, meadow, forest, sands of dark gold, and the faraway, the delicate Southern faraway . . .

I thought then that I had never loved Little Russia as much, that I had never wanted to live as much as I did that autumn. But the only thing I ever talked about was struggling to make a living. All I was learning was barrel-making. Standing in the town square, I decided to visit the Tolstoyans who lived not far from town.

Walking down the mountain to the Podol, I saw many draymen hurriedly driving wagonloads of passengers who had just arrived from the Crimea on the five o'clock train. The mammoth horses were slowly pulling the clattering wagons weighed down with boxes and bales up the hill. And all of this—the smell of candles, vanilla and bast matting, draymen, dust, and people coming from some place nice—made my heart ache once more with a kind of tormented, dreary yet sweet yearning.

I turned off onto a crowded side street which ran between gardens, then walked for some time through the suburb. On summer nights, the "little masters" of the suburb "hooted" wildly, in a marvelous sort of way, all along the valley. In fact, they would sing beautiful, mournful Cossack songs in chorus, harmonizing them as if they were hymns. The "little masters" were threshing right now. At the edge of town, where blue-and-white cottages with clay walls stood in the meadow at the entrance to the valley, flails were flashing on threshing floors. In the valley's calm, the weather was just as hot as it was in town. I hurriedly climbed the mountain to the open, flat steppe.

It was quiet, peaceful, wide-open there. Wherever I looked, the entire steppe was gold with thick, tall stubble. A deep layer of dust lay on the broad, endless road—it seemed I was walking in velvet shoes. And everything all around— the stubble, the road, the air—everything shone from the light of the low evening sun. A middle-aged Ukrainian man with a black suntan passed me. Wearing heavy boots, a sheepskin cap, and thick overcoat the color of rye bread, he was swinging a cane glittering like glass in the sun. The wings of crows flying over the stubble also glittered. You had to lower the brim of your hot hat over your eyes to shield them against this brightness and intense heat. Far away, almost on the horizon, you could make out a wagon being pulled slowly by a team of oxen. You could even see the caretaker's house on the melon fields . . . Ah, it really was glorious here in this silence, this expanse! Yet every bit of my heart wanted to go to the south, beyond the valley, where she had gone away . . .

Half a *verst* from the road, above the valley, the tile-roof of a small farmhouse appeared red. The house belonged to the Tolstoyans, the brothers Pavel and Viktor Timchenko. I walked up to it through the dry, prickly stubble. The place was deserted. I glanced into a small window—only flies, legions of flies, were buzzing inside. They were swarming on the windows, the ceiling, in earthenware pots that were sitting on the shelves. No one seemed to be in the cow shed adjoining the house. The gates were open. The sun had dried the manure heaped in the front yard.

"Where are you going?" a female voice suddenly asked me. I turned around. On the cliff overlooking the valley, Olga Semyonova was sitting at the edge of a melon field. She was the wife of the older Timchenko. Without getting up, she reached her hand to me, and I sat beside her.

"You bored?" I asked, grew quiet, and looked her straight in the face.

She gazed down at her bare feet. Small, suntanned, wearing a dirty shirt and an old skirt, she resembled a little girl sent to guard the melon fields who has sadly spent a long, sunny day at her task. Her face was that of a teenage girl from a Russian village. But no matter how hard I tried, I could not get used to her clothes, to her bare feet which had been walking through manure and prickly stubble. I was actually ashamed to look at those feet. In fact, she tucked them under her, then tucked them even more as she kept looking at her jagged toenails. Yet her feet were small and beautiful.

"My husband went to the meadow to thresh," she said, "and Viktor Nikolaich drove to . . . They arrested Pavlovsky again for refusing to be drafted. You remember Pavlovsky, don't you?"

"I remember," I said automatically.

We grew silent, and for a long time looked at the dark-blue valley, at the forests, sands, and the distance which called out with melancholy. The sun warmed us yet. Round, heavy watermelons lay among long, yellowed whips. Tangled like snakes, they too warmed themselves in the sun.

"Why are you being so cold?" I began. "Why are you so formal? You love me."

She huddled, tucked her feet tighter, and partially closed her eyes. Then she blew away a strand of hair that had fallen on her cheek and said with a resolute smile:

"Give me a cigarette."

I gave her one. She took about two drags, began coughing, tossed the cigarette far away, then thought a while.

"I've been sitting here like this ever since morning," she said. "Chickens come over from the meadow to peck the

29

watermelons . . . I don't know why you think it's so boring here. I like it very, very much . . . "

Above the valley, about two *versts* from the farm, I sat down and took off my hat. I looked through my tears into the distance. And I dreamed of somewhere far away, of sultry Southern towns, of a blue evening on the steppe, of the image of a certain woman that blended with the girl I loved. But I endowed that woman with my own feelings of mystery, and added the childish sorrow I had seen in the eyes of the small woman in the melon field . . .

[1901]

A New Year

"DID YOU HEAR THAT?"
my wife asked. "I'm scared."

It was winter, a moonlit night. Traveling from the South
to Petersburg, we were staying in a manor house in Tambov
province. We were sleeping in the nursery, the only warm
room in the entire house. As I opened my eyes, I saw a faint
twilight tinged with blue, the floor covered with saddle
cloth, and a white stove-bench. I could see a bright, snowy
courtyard above the square window. The stubble of a straw
roof silvered by hoarfrost jutted out. It was the kind of
quietness one finds only in the fields on late winter nights.

"You're sleeping," my wife said unhappily. "I was dozing in the sleigh before we got here, but now I can't . . ."

She was propped up on a large, antique bed against the
opposite wall. When I came to her, she began talking in a
gay whisper:

"You're not mad I woke you, are you? I got a little scared.
But it wasn't all bad. I felt we were totally, totally alone
here, and then suddenly got as scared as a child . . ."

She looked up, then listened carefully for any noises.

"Do you hear how still it is?" she asked almost inaudibly.
I thought of the snowy fields around us. We were sur-

rounded by the dead silence of a Russian winter night which was mysteriously bringing in the New Year. I hadn't spent a night in the countryside for such a long time. For so long, my wife and I hadn't had a moment's peace with each other. I now kissed her eyes, her hair, kissed her repeatedly with that tranquil love which occurs only in rare moments. And she suddenly responded with the impetuous kisses of a girl in love. Then for a long while, she pressed my hand to her burning cheek.

"How good it is!" she said with a sigh, with conviction. She grew silent, then added, "Yes, you are still closer to me than anyone else! Do you feel I love you?"

I squeezed her hand.

"How did it happen?" she asked, opening her eyes. "I didn't marry for love. We don't get along. You say I'm the reason you lead a vulgar, painful existence . . . And yet more and more, we feel we need each other. What's the reason for this? Why does it last for only a few minutes? Happy New Year, Kostya!" she said, trying to smile. And several heavy teardrops fell on my hand.

With her head on the pillow, she began weeping. The tears really did make her attractive as she looked up now and then, smiled through them, and kissed my hand—trying to make it all last longer. I smoothed her hair, letting her know that her tears meant so much to me, that I understood them. I recalled the previous New Year, which we had celebrated as usual in Petersburg with a group of my military colleagues. I wanted to remember the New Year before that, but couldn't. And I again began thinking about what so often had been on my mind—years merging into one formless, monotonous year burdened with gray workdays. Atrophy of the intellect and spirit. Hopes which more and more seemed unattainable, hopes of having my own place, settling somewhere in the country or in the South, spending leisure time in vineyards with my wife and children, catching fish in the summer sea . . . I recalled that exactly a year before, my wife had been worrying with pretended politeness and making a fuss over our New Year's guests who considered us their friends. I remembered how she had smiled at several young guests and proposed enigmatically melancholy toasts. I recalled how distant, how unpleasant she had been to me in the crowded little Petersburg apartment.

"All right, Olya, enough!" I said.

"Give me a handkerchief," she answered quietly—like a child—and breathed with broken sighs. "I'm not crying anymore."

Like an ethereal, silver strip, the moonlight fell on the stove-bench. It appeared strange, brightly pale. Everything else was in semi-darkness—my cigarette smoke drifted in it. And the saddle cloth on the floor, the warm, pale stove-bench—everything breathed with the isolation of country living, the coziness of an old family home.

"Are you glad we came here?" I asked.

"Awfully glad, Kostya, awfully so!" she answered with impetuous sincerity. "I thought about it after you'd gone to sleep. In my opinion," she said, already smiling, "a person should get married twice. Seriously, how happy that would be—standing at the altar knowing exactly what you're doing, having already lived and suffered with your partner! And to live forever at home, in your own place, somewhere far away from everyone . . . 'To be born, to live, and to die in the family home'—that's what Maupassant said!"

She thought a while, then rested her head on the pillow.

"It was Sainte-Beuve," I said.

"Who cares, Kostya? Maybe I'm as dumb as you're always saying, but I'm still the only one who loves you . . . Do you want to go for a walk?"

"A walk? Where to?"

"Just around the courtyard. I'll put on my felt boots, your sheepskin coat . . . You mean you really could sleep now?"

A half an hour later, we were dressed and stood at the door smiling.

"You're not mad, are you?" my wife asked as she took my hand.

She looked affectionately into my eyes. Her face was extraordinarily sweet. All of her seemed so feminine in the soft felt boots which made her shorter, in the gray shawl she had wrapped around her head the way peasant women do.

We walked from the nursery into the corridor, which was dark and cold—like a cellar. In the darkness, we glanced into the parlor and living room as we passed into the front hallway. The squeak of the parlor door rang throughout the house. And from the pale darkness of a large, empty room, two high windows overlooking the garden glanced down at us like enormous eyes. The third window was covered with broken shutters.

"Ai-i-i!" my wife exclaimed at the doorway.

"Don't get so excited," I said. "Better look in there to see that everything's all right."

She calmed down, and we walked timidly into the room. From the windows, we could see a thin, low garden. Actually, we saw bushes scattered all over the broad, snowy clearing. Half the garden was in the house's shadow. Beneath the starry sky of a quiet winter night, the half in the moonlight was pale-white—distinct, delicate. A cat—who knows how it got here—suddenly jumped from a window-sill and landed with a soft thud. We caught a glimpse of it as it stood at our feet shining its orange-gold eyes. I was startled, and my wife asked in a worried voice, "Would you be scared to be here all by yourself?"

Clinging to each other, we passed through the parlor into the living room toward the French doors leading to the balcony. An immense couch, the one I used to sleep on when I came here as a student, was still there in the room. Those summer days seemed like only yesterday, when the entire family had eaten dinner on the balcony. Now, the living room smelled of mould and winter dampness. Heavy, frozen strips of wallpaper hung from the walls. It was painful. I didn't want to think of the past, especially in the presence of this beautiful winter night. From the living room, we could see the whole garden and the plain of snowy white beneath the starry sky. We could see every drift of pure, virginal snow, every little fir tree standing in the whiteness.

"You'll sink there without snowshoes," I said to my wife when she asked me to walk with her through the garden to the barn. "Once, there were winters when I'd sit for nights on end on threshing-floors, in stacks of oats. Right now, the hares are probably getting as close as the balcony."

I tore off a large piece of wallpaper that hung awkwardly by the door and threw it in a corner. Then we went back into the front hallway, through the large timber-paneled vestibule, and out into the frosty air. I sat on a porch step and lit a cigarette. Crunching across the snow in her felt boots, my wife ran down to the snowdrifts and looked up at the moon. Near the horizon, the moon was standing above the long black *izba* where the driver who had brought us from the railway station and the groundskeeper himself were sleeping.

"The moon, the moon!" she said whirling around like a little girl on the broad white courtyard. "It's a golden crescent you see, but it's golden money to me!"

Her voice rang out sharply. It seemed so strange in the silence of the dead estate. Twirling around and around, she crossed over to the driver's covered sleigh, black in the shadow of the *izba*. I could hear her mumbling:

> Tatyana in an open dress
> Onto the wide courtyard is going,
> A mirror to the moon she's showing,
> But in the mirror's darkness soon
> Trembles only the mournful moon . . .

"Never again will I be able to guess who my intended will be!" she said, returning to the porch, puffing gaily in the

35

frosty freshness. She sat on the step next to me. "You didn't fall asleep did you, Kostya? Can I sit next to you, sweetheart, precious?"

A large red dog lumbered up to us from behind the porch. With affectionate condescension, it wagged its fluffy tail. My wife hugged the broad neck thick with fur. The dog looked over her head with intelligent, questioning eyes, with such tender indifference that even it probably didn't know its tail was wagging. I too patted this thick, cold, glossy fur, looked at the moon's pale, human face, at the long black *izba,* the courtyard shining in the snow, and thought optimistically, "Come to think of it, is everything really lost? Who knows what this New Year will bring?"

"What's going on in Petersburg now?" my wife asked as she looked up and gently pushed the dog aside. "What are you thinking about, Kostya?" she asked, moving her face closer to mine. Her face had become younger in the frosty air.

"I'm thinking that peasants never celebrate the New Year, that people all over Russia have been asleep now for so long . . ."

But I didn't want to talk. It was already cold—the frosty air had penetrated my clothing. To our right, through the gates, we saw a field shining like golden mica. We saw a barren traveler's-joy with pale, thin branches. It stood far off in the field and seemed like a glass tree from some fairy tale. During the day, I had seen the skeleton of a dead cow there. The dog now suddenly pricked its ears and raised them sharply. In the distance, something small, something dark was running from the traveler's-joy along the shiny mica. Maybe it was a fox. And in the intense silence, the faint, mysterious crunching of the snow's frozen crust slowly died away.

Listening carefully, my wife asked, "But what if we stayed here?"

I thought a while, then replied, "But wouldn't you get bored?"

And as soon as I had said it, both of us felt we couldn't stand staying here even a year. To leave people, never seeing anything but this snowy field! Suppose we did settle here . . . But what kind of life would that be in the pitiful remains of the estate, on a hundred *dessyatinas* of land? And there were estates just like this all around. Within a hundred *versts* of this place, there wasn't a single house where you could feel any life! And in the countryside itself—famine . . .

We slept soundly. In the morning, both of us rose quickly to leave. When the runners of the sleigh began creaking outside the window of our room, when we could see the tall team of horses passing along snowdrifts, my wife—half awake—smiled sadly. I could sense she was sorry to leave this warm room in the country.

"And so the New Year's here!" I thought, looking out from the squeaking sleigh covered with hoarfrost, looking out onto the gray field. "How will we get through these new three hundred and sixty-five days?"

But the tinkle of sleigh bells confused my thoughts. It was unpleasant to think about the future. Looking out of the sleigh, I was already barely able to make out the estate's lackluster, gray-blue landscape. It rapidly grew smaller in the flat, snowy steppe, gradually blended with the misty faraway of a frosty, foggy day.

The driver shouted at the frost-covered horses and stood up. He appeared to be oblivious to the New Year, to the empty field, to his fate and to our own. He struggled for his pocket under his heavy cloth coat, then under his sheepskin coat. He took out a pipe, and I quickly smelled the aroma of gray, fragrant tobacco smoke. It was a native smell, a pleasant smell. And I was touched by the memory of the manor, of my temporary reconciliation with my wife, who was now dozing, huddled in a corner of the sleigh. Her large eyelashes were gray with frost. Yet in obeying an inner desire to lose myself as quickly as possible in petty worries and life as usual, I cried out with forced gaiety, "Hurry up, Stepan, hurry up! We're late!"

And far ahead, the foggy silhouettes of telegraph poles were running along. And the tinkle of sleigh bells interrupted my thoughts, thoughts of the disjointed, senseless life which awaited me there . . .

[1901]

Gentle Breathing

IN A CEMETERY, ABOVE a fresh mound of clay, stands a new oak cross. It is strong, heavy, smooth.

April. Gray days. From a distance, the tombstones of the spacious district cemetery can yet be seen through naked trees. And the cold wind continually clanks the porcelain wreath at the base of the cross.

A rather large, convex, porcelain medallion is set into the cross. Within the medallion is a photograph of a young schoolgirl, a girl with extraordinary eyes full of joy and life.

It is Olya Meshcherskaya.

As a young girl, she had in no way stood out from the crowd of little brown dresses. What could you say about her other than she was one of many nice, wealthy, happy little girls, that she had ability, that she didn't pay the least bit of attention to the scoldings of her form mistress? And then she began to blossom, to develop not with each passing day, but with each hour. At the age of fourteen, she had a thin waist, slender legs, clearly noticeable breasts, and all those charming curves which words have never been able to fully describe.

By the age of fifteen, she was already known as a beauty.

How painstakingly some of her girl friends combed their hair, how neat they were, how carefully they controlled their impulses! Yet Olya Meshcherskaya was afraid of nothing—neither ink spots on her fingers, a red face, tousled hair, nor exposing her knees as she feel down running.

Carefree, effortlessly, she inconspicuously developed qualities during her last two years of school which set her apart from all the other girls—elegance, grace, cleverness, and the clear sparkle of her eyes. No one could dance like Olya Meshcherskaya, no one could skate like she. At dances, the boys paid more attention to her than to any other girl. And for some reason none of her classmates was as loved by the younger girls. Imperceptibly, she became a young woman, and imperceptibly her fame spread throughout the school. Already, word was that she was flighty, that she could not live without boyfriends, that the Gymnasium student Shenshin had fallen madly in love with her, that she may have loved him, but had been so fickle that he'd tried to commit suicide . . .

During the last winter of her life, Olya Meshcherskaya had been "madly gay," as they said at school. The winter had been snowy, sunny, and frosty. The sun would set early in the evening behind the grove of tall fir trees in the school's snowy garden. The sun was invariably serene and radiant, always promising frost and sun for the following day, promising a stroll down Cathedral Street, skating in the public park, a pink evening, music, and that crowd of skaters which glided in all directions, the crowd in which Olya Meshcherskaya seemed the happiest, most carefree girl.

One day, during the afternoon recess, some blissfully squealing first-graders were chasing her through the assembly hall. While racing as if carried along on a whirlwind, she was unexpectedly summoned to the headmistress's office. She immediately stopped running, took a deep breath, straightened her hair with a quick motion of the hand—the way women do—tugged the corners of her apron up to her shoulders, and with shining eyes ran upstairs. The headmistress was a young-looking woman with gray hair. Sitting at a desk beneath a portrait of the Tsar, she was calmly knitting.

"*Bonjour,* Mademoiselle Meshcherskaya," she said, not looking up from her knitting. "Unfortunately, this is not the first time I have had to call you here to discuss your behavior."

"I'm minding, Madame," Meshcherskaya replied as she walked to the desk and looked at the headmistress with clear, animated eyes, yet with no expression on her face. And she curtsied easily and gracefully, as only she know how.

"You are not minding very well. Unfortunately, I am certain of that," the headmistress said. She gave the thread a tug, and the ball of yarn barely unwound on the polished floor. Meshcherskaya watched it with curiosity. "I shall not repeat myself," the headmistress said. "I shall not be verbose."

Meshcherskaya loved this unusually clean, large study. On frosty days, it smelled of the bright, warm tile stove and the fresh lilies of the valley on the desk. She looked at the young tsar, painted standing in some splendid hall. She looked at the straight part in the white, even waves of the headmistress's hair, and waited expectantly.

"You are no longer a little girl," the headmistress said in a tone of great significance while concealing her growing irritation.

"Yes, Madame," Meshcherskaya answered simply, almost gaily.

"But neither are you a woman yet," the headmistress continued in a tone of even greater significance as her luster-less face turned slightly crimson. "In the first place, what kind of hairdo is that? It is a woman's hairdo!"

"It's not my fault, Madame, if I have nice hair," Meshcherskaya answered, softly touching her beautiful hairdo with both hands.

"Ah, there you are! You are not at fault!" the headmistress said. "You are not to blame for the hairdo, for these expensive combs, for bankrupting your parents with twenty-ruble shoes! But, I repeat, you are completely losing sight of the fact that you are still only a schoolgirl . . . "

And then with the same simplicity and calmness, Meshcherskaya suddenly, yet politely interrupted the headmistress:

"Pardon me, Madame, but you're wrong. I am a woman. And do you know who is to blame? My papa's friend and neighbor, your own brother—Alexei Mikhailovich Malyutin. It happened last summer in the country . . . "

A month after this conversation, a Cossack officer—a homely, plebeian-looking sort having absolutely nothing in common with Olya Meshcherskaya's circle of friends—shot her on the platform of a railway station while surrounded by a large crowd of people who had just gotten off the train. And the subsequent investigation confirmed the improbable, stunning confession Olya Meshcherskaya had made to the headmistress. The officer told the police investigator that Meshcherskaya had enticed him, seduced him, and promised to marry him. But on the day of the murder when she was seeing him off at the railway station as he was leaving for Novocherkassk, she suddenly told him that she had never seriously considered loving him, that everything she had said about marriage was only her way of mocking him. And then she gave him one of the small pages from her diary to read, the page which told of Malyutin.

"I skimmed the sentences," the officer said. "And right away, right then as she was walking around on the platform waiting for me to finish, I shot her. The diary is right here. See for yourself what she wrote for July 10th of last year."

Meshcherskaya had written the following:

"It is now two o'clock in the morning. I fell sound asleep, but suddenly woke up. I became a woman today! Papa, Mama, and Tolya all drove to town, and I was left alone. I was so happy to be by myself! In the morning, I strolled in the garden, the fields, the woods. It seemed I was the only person in the whole wide world. I had such pleasant thoughts, thoughts I'd never had before. I even ate dinner alone. Then I played the piano for a whole hour. The music made me feel like I'd live forever, that I'd be happier than anyone had ever been. Then I fell asleep in Papa's study. Katya woke me at four o'clock. She said that Alexei Mikhailovich had arrived. I was so glad to see him, so pleased to greet and entertain him. He came on his team of Vyatka horses. They stood the whole time by the porch. He stayed because it was raining, and wanted the roads to dry out before he left by evening. He was sorry Papa wasn't at home. He was very lively and treated me like a queen, joking all the time that he had been in love with me for ever so long.

"When we were walking in the garden just before tea, the weather was again lovely. The sun shone through the wet garden, even though it had become really cold. He walked with his arm in mine, saying he was Faust with Marguerite. He's fifty-six, but still handsome and always so well dressed. The only thing I didn't like was that he was wearing a loose cape. He smelled of English cologne, his eyes were black, youthful, and his beard parted elegantly into two long halves—all the color of silver.

"We drank our tea while sitting on the glass veranda. I didn't feel very well and lay down on the ottoman. He smoked, then came over and sat down beside me. He again started paying me all kinds of compliments, then looked closely at my hand and kissed it. I covered my face with a silk handkerchief. He kissed my lips several times through the scarf...I don't understand how it could have happened. I must have been crazy. I never thought I was that

43

kind of girl! Now there's only one thing left for me to do . . . I despise him so much I can't stand it! . . . ''

This April, the town has become clean, dry. Its stones have turned white, and are easy and pleasant to walk on. Each Sunday after the church service, a small woman dressed in mourning, wearing black kid gloves and carrying an ebony parasol, walks out of town along Cathedral Street. The street gradually becomes a highway as it crosses a dirt square crowded with coal-faced blacksmiths. There, fresh winds blow in from the fields. As she continues on her way, the cloudy, sloping sky and the spring fields which can be seen between the monastery wall and jail appear gray. And then, as you pass the puddles by the monastery wall and turn off to the left, you will see what seems to be a large, low garden surrounded by a white fence. Above the gates is the inscription ''The Assumption of Our Lady.''

The small woman gently crosses herself and walks automatically along the main path lined with trees. She approaches the bench which faces the oak cross and sits there for an hour, two hours, sits there in the wind, the spring cold. She sits until her feet in their light-weight boots, her hands in their narrow kid gloves begin to shiver. Listening to the spring birds singing sweetly in the cold, listening to the sound of the wind blowing the porcelain wreath, she sometimes thinks she would give half her life if that wreath would only disappear. This wreath, this mound, this cross of oak! Is it possible that she lies below, the girl whose eyes shine with immortality from the porcelain medallion on that cross? And how can one explain this look of innocence after hearing the horrible stories now associated with the name of Olya Meshcherskaya? Yet in the depths of her heart, the small woman is happy, happy like those people devoted to some kind of passionate dream.

The woman is Olya Meshcherskaya's form mistress. She is still young but has lived for a long time with whatever

44

fantasy she has substituted for reality. Her first fantasy was her brother, a poor ensign who was quite ordinary. His life became her life. His future, which for some reason she thought so brilliant, became hers as well. When he was killed at Mukden, she convinced herself that she was now a woman working for noble goals. For her, Olya Meshcherskaya's death is a new, fascinating dream. Her thoughts, her emotions are continually focused now on Olya Meshcherskaya. Every holiday, she walks to the girl's grave. For hours, she doesn't take her eyes from the oak cross as she remembers the pale little face of Olya Meshcherskaya in the coffin among the flowers. And she remembers a conversation she once heard. It was during the afternoon recess. Strolling through the school garden, Olya Meshcherskaya was chattering to her best girl friend, the tall, plump Subbotina:

"In one of Papa's books—he's got lots of real old, funny books—I read what a beautiful woman should look like . . . You've got to understand that so much was written there that you just couldn't remember it all. Well, naturally, it said she should have black eyes boiling like pitch. Really and truly, that's what it said—'boiling like pitch'! Eyelashes black as night. A blush 'that plays gently on the cheek.' A thin waist. Hands longer than normal. Get it? Longer than normal! Small feet. Fairly large breasts. Nicely rounded calves. Knees the color of mother-of-pearl. Sloping shoulders. I've learned a lot of it by heart, since it's so true! But do you know what's the most important thing of all? Gentle breathing! And I've got it—just listen to how I breathe. It's true, isn't it?"

Now this gentle breathing has once again vanished into the world. Into this cloudy sky. Into this cold wind of spring.

[1916]

The Passing

THE PRINCE DIED BEFORE evening on August 29th. He died as he had lived—silently, aloof.

The sun, shining golden just before dusk, retreated now and then behind ethereal, darkish storm clouds stretching like islands above the distant fields to the west. The wind was easy, calm. The estate's broad courtyard was empty. Everything was very quiet in the house, as if it were all the more responsible for the summer.

The beggars wandering the countryside had already learned of the prince's death. They appeared near the dilapidated stone columns at the entrance of the estate and began singing out of tune the ancient sacred verse "On the Passing of the Soul from the Body." There were three of these beggars—a pockmarked fellow wearing a light-blue shirt with shortened sleeves, an old man standing tall and straight, and a suntanned girl of about fifteen who had already become a mother. She stood there with the sleepy child in her arms, holding her small breast to his sucking mouth, and singing loudly, without feeling. Both peasant men were blind from cataracts. The girl's eyes were clear and dark.

Doors slammed in the house. Natasha jumped out onto the front porch and rushed like a whirlwind across the courtyard to the servants' quarters. The wall clock could be heard from the open house slowly striking six. A moment later, a field hand was already on the run, putting on his cloth coat while racing to saddle the horse and then gallop to the village to get the old women. The pilgrim Anyuta, whose short hair made her look like a boy, had been visiting the estate. Leaning from a small window of the servants' quarters, she clapped her hands and shouted something to the field hand, something meaningless, inarticulate, intensely joyful.

When the young Bestuzhev entered the dead man's room, the deceased was lying on his back on an antique walnut bed. He was covered with an old blanket of red satin. The collar of his nightshirt was unbuttoned, his eyes were half-closed, motionless, as if he were drunk. His head was tilted back. The dark face, unshaven for so long, the face with its large, grizzled moustache, had grown pale.

On the prince's orders, the shutters of this room had been closed all summer. Now they were being opened. A candle was burning with a yellow glow on the chest of drawers near the bed. His heart pounding, Bestuzhev looked down over his shoulder and stared greedily at the strange thing which had already grown cold and now sunk into the bed.

The shutters were being opened one after the other. The distant sunset, appearing orange as it burned away in the storm clouds, peered into the windows through the dark branches of pine trees standing in the front garden. Leaving the dead man, Bestuzhev opened one of these windows wide. He could feel pure air being drawn into the room, into the stagnating smell of medicines. The tearful Natasha walked in and began carrying out everything the prince—suddenly seized the previous week by some sort of anxious greed—had ordered brought in and laid before him on the tables and armchairs. An old Cossack saddle. Bridles. A brass hunting

47

horn. Dog leashes. A cartridge belt. No longer afraid of ringing the bridle bits or clanging the stirrups against each other, she carried everything with a hardened, austere look on her face. She was breathing heavily in the candlelight as she passed the chest of drawers.

The prince was motionless. So were his half-closed eyes, squinting slightly. The room was filled with the river freshness blending with the dry warmth of the evening. The sun died out, faded away. The pine branches of the front garden grew coldly dark above the limpid sea far to the west. From above, the sea appeared greenish. From below, it was the color of saffron. The chirping of a little bird outside the window seemed somehow very unpleasant.

"Why should anyone feel sorry for him?" Natasha said in a serious voice as she returned to the room, opened a dresser drawer and took out clean underwear, sheets, and a pillowcase. "He died peacefully. God grant that everyone could die just as peacefully. And there's nobody to feel sorry for him. He didn't have anyone," she added, then left the room again.

Sitting on the windowsill, Bestuzhev kept looking into the dark corner at the bed on which the dead man was lying. Bestuzhev was still trying to understand something, to collect his thoughts, feel a sense of horror. Yet there was no horror. He felt only amazement, the impossibility of comprehending what had happened. Was everything really all over now? Could people in this bedroom now talk as freely as Natasha was doing? Yet, Bestuzhev thought, she had been talking the same way about the prince for more than a month, as if he were already no longer among the living.

In the twilight, he could smell a faint, unusually pleasant smoke drifting in from the courtyard. It had a soothing effect. It spoke of the earth, of ordinary human life which continued to go on. He could hear the steady churning of a water wheel coming from the darkened meadows by the river. A week earlier, the prince had been sitting on an old millstone near the gates leading to the mill. Thin, ashen-faced, wearing a cap and a tight fox-fur coat, he had been sitting bent over, leaning his hands against the gray, porous rock. An old man brought some rye to grind. While undoing his sack, he squinted and looked up from under his eyebrows at the prince. "You've gotten so skinny!" he said coldly, contemptuously. Until then, he'd always addressed the prince with respect. "There's really nothin' you can do!" he said. "No, you ain't got much time left. Ain't you goin' on seventy?"

"Fifty-one," the prince said.

"Fifty one!" the old man repeated derisively as he fussed with the sack. "Can't be," he said stubbornly. "You're lots older than me."

"You're a fool," the prince said with a smile. "After all, we grew up together."

"So we grew up together, so we didn't grow up together. All the same, you ain't got much time left," the old man said while straining to lift the bushel of rye, then pressing it to this chest. Squatting under its heavy load, he rushed down to the noisy mill which was white with flour.

"Now you're going away, little master," Natasha said impassively, yet in a tone of significance, as she carried in a bucket of hot water.

Bestuzhev was suddenly terrified by this bucket, by these words. He got up from the windowsill and without looking at Natasha strode through the front hallway leading from the dead man's room onto the black porch. Yevgeniya and Agafya, two old women who had driven in from the village, were washing their hands in the semi-darkness near the porch. One was pouring water from a pitcher, the other leaning over, pulling the hem of her skirt up to her knees, wringing it out, then shaking her fingers. These old women were even more terrifying. Bestuzhev rushed past them in the dry garden already losing its autumn leaves. From where he stood, the garden seemed to shine mysteriously in the light of the round, enormous, mirror-like moon which had just appeared among the trunks of faraway trees.

By nine o'clock, the room where the prince had died was in order. Everything had been cleaned up. The bed was gone. The cleaned floors had a warm smell. Tables had been placed at an angle in a corner near the door. They were near a window—the upper pane turned silver in the moonlight. On the tables, a sheet draped the body, which seemed to be very large. Three fat candles in tall church candlesticks were burning transparently at the head of the deceased—they flickered with crystalline smoke.

Tishka, the son of Semyon the churchwarden, was reading the Psalter aloud. He read it mournfully, yet hurriedly. Scrubbed clean, he had combed his hair and was wearing a new coat. "Praise the Lord on High," he intoned, imitating the monks. "Praise Him all His angels, praise Him all His hosts . . . " Transparent tongues of golden flame, bright-blue at their base, flickered on the candles with a dark smokiness.

The only fire that had been started in the house was in the butler's room. A table was standing in there beneath a window. A samovar was boiling on the table. People were drinking tea. Natasha and Yevgeniya were there, pale and serious, wearing black shawls, looking like Death. The mournfully humble Agafya. Grigory the carpenter, who had already begun making the coffin in the barn. Semyon the churchwarden, an old man with dull, lead-colored eyes ruined from continual reading in the flickering candlelight of the dead. Semyon, who was supposed to relieve his son, had brought along his own book. It was bound in a coarse, stiff, brown-leather cover smudged with drops of wax. Here and there, the corners of pages had been burned.

"No matter how bad your life is, it'll still be hard to leave this world," Agafya said sadly while pouring tea from her cup into her saucer.

"Everyone knows it'll be hard," Grigory said. "If he'd known, if he hadn't lived the way he did, he should have destroyed everything he owned. But then we're afraid to let our estate go. You're always thinking that when you get old there won't be any place for you to go . . . But see, he didn't live to be an old man!"

"Our life is like a wave," Semyon said. "Death, they say, must be met with joy and trembling."

"It is a transfiguration, my dear, not death," Yevgeniya corrected him in a dry, moralizing tone.

"With trembling or not with trembling, no one wants to die," Grigory said. "Even a bug is scared of death. That means they've got souls too."

"Not a soul, dear boy, but an empty hole," Yevgeniya said, sermonizing even more.

Finishing his last cup, Semyon shook his head, brushed back the sweaty, dark-gray hair from his forehead, stood up, made the sign of the cross, grabbed the Psalter, and tiptoed through the dark parlor, then through the dark living room to the deceased.

"Off with you, be off with you, my dear," Yevgeniya said to him as he was leaving. "Yes, read with greater feeling. When someone reads well, the sins fall from a sinner like leaves from a dry tree."

Relieving Tishka, Semyon put his glasses on, looked severely through them, gently picked at the wax which had spilled over from the candles, slowly crossed himself, opened the book resting on the lectern, and began reading softly, affectionately, with a sorrowful persuasiveness, raising his voice in warning only occasionally.

The hallway door near the black porch was open. While he was reading, Semyon could hear feet stamping on the porch. Two girls had come to view the deceased. Both were dressed up and wearing new shoes. They tiptoed into the room timidly and joyfully, whispering back and forth. Crossing themselves and trying to tread softly, one of them—her breasts quivering under a new pink blouse— approached the table and pulled back the sheet from the prince's face. The candlelight fell on the blouse. In this light, the girl's frightened face became pale and red. And the prince's dead face began shining with the color of bone. The large, grizzled moustache, which had grown out during his illness, was already letting the light shine through. There was a certain dark wateriness in his half-open eyes . . .

Tishka was avidly smoking a cigarette in the passageway while waiting for the girls to come out. They slipped past pretending not to notice him. One ran from the porch. He managed to grab the other, the girl in the pink blouse. She tore herself from him, whispering:

"Hey, are you crazy! Let me go! I'll tell your father . . . "

Tishka let her go. She ran off into the garden. The moon—already small, white, clear—was high above the dark garden. In its light, the cold iron roof of the bathhouse shone like gold. The girl turned around in the shade of the garden, looked at the sky, and exclaimed:

"Goodness, what a night!"

And her happy voice rang out in the still of the night with a charming, joyful tenderness.

III

Bestuzhev paced the courtyard from one end to the other. Standing in the courtyard—empty, broad, and shining in the moonlight—he could see the glimmerings of the village beyond the river, then the lighted windows of the servants' quarters, where he heard the murmurings of people eating supper. The doors of the barn were open. Inside, a broken lantern was burning as it rested on the driver's seat of a carriage. Leaning over with one leg up, Grigory was plan- ing a board that was lying on an old sawhorse. The lantern flickered with a smoky-red glow, casting shadows in the barn's faint light. As Bestuzhev paused at the barn door, Grigory looked up in excitement and said with good-natured pride:

"I'm already working on the lid . . . "

Later, Bestuzhev stood a while at an open window of the servants' quarters resting his elbows on the sill. The cook was clearing the table, wiping it with a rag. The teenaged boys who tended the sheep were bedding down in the *izba*. Removing his shoes, Mitka was saying his prayers as he knelt on a bunk covered with fresh straw. Vanka was praying in the center of the room. A stove repairman with red, shaggy hair was sitting on a bench and rolling a cigarette out of newspaper. Broad-shouldered and short, he wore a black shirt flecked with slaked lime. He'd come from the village beyond the river to repair the crumbling inside walls of the prince's crypt, and was supposed to begin work the following morning.

Anyuta was babbling in stupid, blissful gibberish from the stove-bench:

"He went and died, Your Excellency, and he didn't provide anything for me . . . Didn't give me a thing . . . Nothing at all, you wait and you wait . . . Now keep on waiting . . . Keep on waiting . . . Wait now! Did you wait, dear? Did he think of me? Now has he understood what those candles are doing there at his head, the stupid man? If only someone would give just two little rubles to cover my body! I'm a cripple, a freak. I don't have anybody. Look at my breast!'

And she tore open her blouse and bared her breast.

"Totally naked. Just like you, you stupid man! And even when I was old I loved you. I yearned for you. You were handsome, gay, tender. A pure young lady! You wasted away in your grief, wasted your youth on your Lyudmi-lochka. Stupid man, she only tortured you, tormented you, yes, even went off and married somebody else. I'm the only one who really loved you, but only my pillow knew it! I'm a

53

cripple, a freak, but I've got a soul, maybe the soul of an angel, maybe an archangel. I alone loved you, and I alone am glad you are dead . . . "

And she began to laugh and cry wildly, joyously.

"Anyuta, let's go read from the Psalter," the repairman said loudly in the tone people use to calm children. "Go now. You're not afraid, are you?"

"Fool! If my legs were all right, I'd go. Is that wrong?" Anyuta bawled through her tears. "They're afraid of their sins, the sins of the dead. They're saints, immaculate they are!"

"But I'm not afraid," the repairman said in a carefree manner, lighting a cigarette that burned with a green glow. "If only for a night, I'll lie with you in the family crypt . . . "

Anyuta sobbed ecstatically, wiping her tears with her blouse.

The faint shadows of white storm clouds trailing across the moon fell onto the courtyard. They did not disturb the bright, beautiful kingdom of the night, but only made it more beautiful. And the beaming moon rolled over the clouds in the depths of the clear sky, above the shining roof of the dark old house where light was coming from only a corner window, from the candles at the head of the dead prince.

[1918]

Sunstroke

AFTER LUNCH, THEY LEFT THE bright hotness of the dining room, stepped out onto the deck of the steamer, and stopped at the railing. She shut her eyes, leaned her cheek against her closed hand, and laughed a natural, charming laugh—everything about this small woman was charming. And then she said:

"I feel like I've had too much to drink . . . You came from out of the blue. Three hours ago, I didn't even know you existed. I don't even know where you got on. Samara? But it doesn't really matter. Am I getting dizzy, or is the boat turning?"

Darkness and the glow of lights lay ahead. A strong yet gentle wind blew from out of the darkness into their faces, and the lights were vanishing somewhere to the side. Showing off as boats often do on the Volga, the steamer made a wide turn and rushed up to a small pier.

The lieutenant took her hand and raised it to his lips. Small and strong, it had a suntanned aroma. And a feeling of bliss, of terror, almost stopped his heart from beating when he thought how the rest of her body beneath this thin, gingham dress, this body which had spent a whole month lying in the Southern sun on the hot sands of the seashore, was most likely firm and suntanned. She had told him she was traveling from Anapa. The lieutenant mumbled:

"Let's get off here..."

"Get off where?" she asked in astonishment.

"On this pier."

"Why?"

He remained silent. She again leaned her hot cheek against the heel of her hand.

"Madness..."

"Let's get off," he repeated dumbly. "I beg you..."

"Well, do as you please," she said, turning away.

Revving its engines, the steamer gently knocked against the dimly lit pier—the two almost fell on each other. The end of a rope came flying over their heads, then was tugged back, water bubbled noisily, and the gangplank crashed down. The lieutenant rushed to get their things.

In less than a minute, they had passed through the pier's sleepy little waiting room, walked ankle-deep in the sand, and quietly seated themselves in a dusty, horse-drawn cab. It seemed as if it would never end—driving up the mountain's slope on a road made soft by the dust, driving up past the crooked lanterns which appeared from time to time. But then they reached the top, continued on, began crackling along a pavement, crossed some kind of town square past offices and a belfry. On this late night in a district town, even the summer aroma was warm...

The cab driver stopped near a lighted entryway. Through open doors, they could see an old, steep wooden staircase. An elderly, unshaven bellman wearing a pink Russian shirt and frock coat took their things as if displeased and walked ahead on his worn-out feet. The three went into a large room which was unbearably stuffy, having been heated during the day by the sun. The room had white, lowered curtains on the windows. Two candles which had never been lit sat on a dresser backed with a large mirror. As soon as they walked into the room and the bellman had closed the door, the lieutenant bent down violently and both of them lost their breath in a delirious kiss. They kissed as if wanting to remember this moment for years to come. Neither had ever experienced anything like it.

Ten o'clock in the morning, a morning sunny, hot, and happy with the sound of churches, of the marketplace on the square directly in front of the hotel, with the scent of hay, tar, and—once more—all those ineffable smells of a Russian district town. This small woman left, this woman with no name. Wanting to remain anonymous, she had jokingly told him she was simply the "Beautiful Unknown." They had slept very little. But in the morning, after spending but five minutes washing and dressing, she came from behind the screen near the bed. She was fresh as a girl of seventeen. Was she embarrassed? No, she didn't seem to be. Just as before, she was at ease, gay, and—serious.

"No, no, dear," she said when he asked to continue traveling with her. "No, you've got to wait for the next boat. If we leave together, everything would be spoiled. I'd find that very unpleasant. I swear I'm not at all the kind of woman you might think I am. Never before have I ever been involved in anything even remotely resembling what has taken place between the two of us. Indeed, it will never happen again. I just temporarily lost my senses... More than likely, both of us were afflicted with something like a sunstroke... "

And the lieutenant somehow easily agreed. In light-hearted, gay spirits, he rode with her to the pier—just as the Pink Flyer was leaving—kissed her on the cheek in front of everyone on the deck, and was barely able to jump onto the gangplank as it was being pulled back.

He returned to the hotel in the same light-hearted, carefree manner. But even so, things had already changed. The room without her seemed somehow entirely different. It was still filled with her—yet empty. How strange! He could still smell

57

her expensive English cologne. Her half-empty cup was still standing on the tray. Yet she was no longer there . . . And the lieutenant's heart suddenly contracted with a feeling of such tender love that he rushed for a cigarette, then paced the room several times from one end to the other.

"What a strange adventure!" he said aloud, laughing, feeling tears come to his eyes. "I swear I'm not at all the kind of woman you might think I am . . . " And she was already gone . . .

The screen had been moved aside. The bed was still unmade. And he felt that he simply didn't have the strength now to look at it. He put the screen in front of it and closed the windows so he wouldn't hear the voices from the marketplace and the squeaking of wheels. He pulled down the white, bubbling curtains and sat on the divan. Yes, that's the end of this "road adventure"! She's gone. By now, she's far away, probably sitting in the glassed, white observation room or out on the deck looking at the immense river shining in the sunlight, at the barges approaching the steamer, at the yellow sandbars, the sparkling distance of water and sky, at all this vast, Volga expanse. And goodbye, already forever, for always . . . Goodbye, because where would they be able to meet now? "I just couldn't," he thought. "I wouldn't go to that town where her husband is, her three-year old daughter is, her whole family is, where everything that makes up her everyday life is. I wouldn't do it for anything in the world!" It seemed to him that the town was special, in some way off-limits. And he was astounded, actually staggered by the thought that she would live her own solitary life there, would perhaps remember him often, remember their chance encounter, their fleeting encounter, and that he would never ever see her again. No, it just can't be! It's too savage, unnatural, improbable! And he felt such pain, felt so useless while thinking of spending the rest of his life without her, that he was overwhelmed by feelings of horror and despair.

"To hell with it!" he said to himself, got up, and again started pacing the room, trying not to look at the bed behind the screen. "What's the matter with me, anyway? And what's so special about her? After all, what really happened? It was just a sunstroke of some kind! What I should really be worrying about is how I'm going to spend an entire day without her in this hole!"

He again reflected on everything about her down to the smallest detail. He recalled the fragrance of her suntanned skin. Her gingham dress. Her firm body. The lively, natural, gay sound of her voice... He was still experiencing that feeling of having just savored the sweet joy of her female allure. Even now, the sensation was so extraordinarily alive. But now the overriding feeling was this other, totally new sensation—a strange, inexplicable feeling which he hadn't experienced when they had been together, a feeling he could not have imagined the day before when he had started—or so he thought at the time—just an amusing acquaintance. It was a feeling he now couldn't even tell her about! "But the main thing," he thought, "is that now you'll never tell her! What can you do? How are you going to live through this endless day with these memories, this torment without respite, in this godforsaken hick town overlooking the same shining Volga where that pink steamer took her away?"

He had to pull himself together, find something to do, distract himself in some way, go somewhere. He resolutely donned his officer's hat, took his riding crop, hurried down the empty hallway with spurs clanking, and ran down the staircase to the entrance. Well, where to now? A cab driver was standing by the entrance. Young, wearing a comfortable, close-fitting coat, he was calmly smoking a cigarette he had rolled out of newspaper. The lieutenant looked at him in dismay, with amazement. How could a person be sitting so calmly in that driver's seat, how could he be so relaxed, carefree, indifferent? "I'm probably the only one in this whole town who's so miserably unhappy," the lieutenant thought, walking to the marketplace.

The market had dispersed in all directions. He trod on the fresh dung lying among the wagons, among the carts loaded with cucumbers, among new basins and earthenware pots. And the old women sitting on the ground vied with each other in shouting at him, taking pots in their hands and knocking them, thumping them with their fingers, showing off the high quality of their wares. The shouting peasant men deafened him with cries of "Here's the best little cucumbers, Your Grace!" It was all so stupid and ridiculous that he fled the marketplace.

He entered the cathedral, where the faithful were already singing hymns loudly, gaily, resolutely, with the conscientiousness of a duty being fulfilled. He then wandered for a long time, circling the small, hot, neglected little garden standing at the edge of the mountain cliff. It overlooked the blinding bright steel of the river's expanse. The shoulder straps and buttons of his tunic had become too hot to touch. The inside band of his hat was wet with perspiration, his face streaming.

Returning to the hotel, he experienced a feeling of delight as he strode into the large, empty, cool dining room on the first floor. He removed his hat with a sense of great pleasure, and sat at a small table near an open window. The heat came in through the window, yet the breeze was bringing fresh air with it. He ordered an iced pot-herb soup. Everything was good, infinitely happy, and so full of joy. There was joy even in this oppressive heat, in all the smells of the marketplace, throughout this one-horse town so unfamiliar to him. There was a joy even in this old district hotel.

But his heart was breaking all the same. He downed several wine glasses of vodka, tasted some slightly salted dill pickles, and felt that without any hesitation he would die the next day if by some miracle she would return and he could spend another day like today with her. He would spend it with her if only, if only to tell her, to prove to her somehow, to convince her that he loved her with such torment, such ecstasy . . . But why prove It? Why convince her? He didn't know why, yet this seemed more essential to him than life itself.

"My nerves are on edge!" he said, pouring his fifth glass of vodka.

He pushed the soup away, asked for some black coffee, started smoking a cigarette, and thought hard. What should he do now? How could he escape this sudden, unexpected love? Yet he acutely felt that escape was impossible. Suddenly, he again jumped up, took his hat and riding crop, asked where the post office was, and hurried there already knowing what he would say in the telegram: "From now on, until death, my entire life will be forever yours, to do with as you please."

But in approaching the old, thick-walled building which housed the post office and telegraph, he stopped in horror. He knew the name of the town where she lived. He knew she had a husband and three-year-old daughter. Yet he knew neither her last name—nor her first! While they were eating dinner in the hotel restaurant the night before, he had asked her several times what her name was. Each time, she had laughed and said:

"Why do you want to know who I am, what my name is?"

The display window of a photographer's studio was at a corner near the post office. For a long time, he looked at the large portrait of some soldier in thick epaulets, with bulging eyes, a narrow forehead, impressive, magnificent sideburns, and the broadest of chests covered with medals. How savage, how terrible everyday life is when it suffers—yes, he now understood it suffered—from this terrible "sunstroke," from too much love, from too much happiness! He glanced at a couple of newlyweds—a young man wearing a long frock coat and white tie. The man's hair was cut as short as a hedgehog's. He was extending an arm entwined with that of his bride, who had on a wedding veil. The lieutenant shifted his eyes to the portrait of some nice, impetuous lady wearing a student's cap tilted to one side. In despair, tormented by jealousy of all these strangers, these people who were not suffering in the least, he began looking long and hard down the street.

"Where to? What now?"

The street was abandoned. The buildings were all the same—white, two-storied, middle-class, with large gardens, and—it seemed—not a soul in them. A thick white dust lay on the pavement. And all of this was blinded, flooded by that hot, fiery, joyful sunlight which somehow became diffused here. In the distance, the street rose, bent, and leaned against the cloudless, grayish reflection of the horizon. There was something Southern in this reminiscent of Sevastopol, Kerch . . . Anapa. This was particularly hard to take. And with bowed head the lieutenant returned to the hotel, returned squinting in the sunlight, looking with concentration at the ground, weaving, stumbling, catching his spurs against each other.

He returned as exhausted as if he had just completed a long trek somewhere in Turkestan, in the Sahara. Summoning the little strength he had left, he entered his large, empty room. It had already been put back in order, no longer with any trace of her. Only a hairpin which she had forgotten now lay on the night stand!

He pulled off his tunic and looked at himself in the mirror. A typical officer's face. Suntanned gray with a moustache bleached white by the sun. Pale-blue eyes seeming even paler against the sun tan. And this face now had the agitated expression of a madman. There was something about the thin white shirt with its stiffly-starched collar that was both youthful and profoundly unhappy. He lay on his back on the bed with his dusty boots resting on the footboard. The windows were open, the curtains pulled down. From time to time, a light breeze puffed them as it blew in the oppressive heat of hot iron roofs and this Volga world, this world which bore all that light and by now had become empty and silent.

He lay with his hands behind his head and stared straight ahead. Then he clenched his teeth and closed his eyes as he felt tears rolling down his cheeks. At last, he fell asleep. When he again opened his eyes, the evening sun was already turning a reddish yellow behind the curtains. The wind had died down. The room was dry and stuffy, like an oven. And he remembered yesterday and this morning as if they had happened ten years earlier.

He got up slowly, took his time washing, raised the curtains, rang for service, asked for a samovar and his bill. For a long time, he drank tea with lemon. Then ordered a cab. Had the bellman take his things. Sat in the cab, sat on its red, faded seat. Gave the bellman a whole five rubles.

"I'm the same one who brought you here last night, Your Grace!" the cab driver said gaily while taking hold of the reins.

As they drove down to the pier, a summer's night was already turning blue above the Volga. Many multicolored little lights were already scattered along the river. And lights were hung from the masts of a steamer fast approaching.

"I got you here just in time!" the driver said as if angling for a tip.

The lieutenant gave him five rubles, took out his ticket, passed on down to the pier. Just like the previous night, the steamer moored with a gentle knock. There was a slight dizziness caused by the shaking pier, then the flying end of a rope, the sound of water bubbling as it rushed forward from the paddle wheels, which turned gently in reverse. This steamer seemed to be a good one, unusually inviting with its crowd of people, all its decks lit up, and the smells coming from its kitchen.

In less than a minute, they had left, gone up the river in the same direction she had been carried that very morning.

63

■

The somber, drowsy reflection of the dark summer sunset dying away far ahead appeared in the river as a myriad of colors. In the distance, quivering ripples still shone here and there beneath it, beneath this sunset. And the little lights swam and swam behind the boat, vanishing into the surrounding darkness.

The lieutenant sat on the deck beneath a canopy, feeling as if he had aged ten years.

[1925]

The Mordvinian Sarafan

WHY AM I GOING TO SEE HER, this woman I scarcely know? As if everything else weren't enough, she's pregnant. Why did I start, then encourage this useless acquaintance, which is actually repellent? We met last night at Leontyev's, and again the joyous smile, a minute of disconnected, awkward conversation, then a firm handshake and the request:

"Drop by my place whenever you see a light in the window! I'll be glad, really I will. Come by whenever you get the notion. I'm always at home. Come tomorrow, and I'll show you my new Mordvinian sarafan . . . "

And again I'm going. For some reason, I'm even hurrying.

The damp March wind is blowing straight into my face. Moscow rests beneath a black spring night. Up ahead, the street lights shine distinctly. High above the blue-black sky, plump clouds are glowing white from the lights of the city below. Church cupolas twinkling with old gilding become mysteriously lost in that whiteness. And from all directions, the infinite, reddish eyes of buildings are gazing, eyes which seem enormous in the dark.

Again, she has probably been waiting all day, getting

ready. She has gone to buy fruit and cookies, gotten all dressed up. It seems she has always imagined that some day life would suddenly take on some joyful meaning for her, that a "sensitive" man of some sort would appear who could at last value her mind, her soul, which her husband doesn't appreciate. I'm so ashamed thinking about all this that I feel like turning around and running back.

All the same, I'm here at the door of her apartment house. I'm walking in. Without stopping, I'm going up the narrow staircase covered with worn carpet. God, how far up I've got to go, how ridiculous all of this is! But it doesn't make any difference—I've already rung the doorbell. Rapid footsteps on the other side of the door, and it's opened not by the maid, but by the lady herself.

Again, the joyous smile, which for some reason expresses the usual surprise. An instant of mutual confusion, then hasty sentences apparently rehearsed:

"Oh, how nice you kept your promise, saw the light in my window, and dropped by! And I'm totally alone—even let my servant have the night off! After all, you know, they've really gone crazy over those movies . . . Well, sir, take your coat off and let's have some tea . . . "

How eagerly she welcomes this "dropping by"! Besides "take your coat off," a clumsy kiss on my temple when I kiss her hand, and her announcement that the servant has the night off. Although I'm so ashamed I can hardly stand it, I nevertheless stride into the living room as if nothing were the matter and casually wipe my glasses with a handkerchief. While wiping them, I think, "Yes, her hairdo looks nice. She must have had it done at the hairdresser's. That means I was right. She's been waiting, getting ready. And then there's this marsh-green, velvet dress just revealing her large breasts, the pearls between them, the gray silk stockings, the satin slippers . . . "

"Sit down, Peter Petrovich. Right this very minute I'll . . . "

66

And she quickly leaves the room. She's very excited and—
to tell the truth—doesn't look bad at all. Pregnancy has a
special kind of beauty, causing the body to blossom in a
marvelous way. Her lips are already faintly flushed, a little
swollen, yet her eyes are magnificently dark and sparkling.

Sighing, I drop onto the divan. As one would expect, the
setting is quite ordinary. A black piano with its lid up.
Above it, a portrait of a threatening Beethoven with high
cheeks. Nearby, a large lamp resting on a tall base beneath
an immense pink lampshade. A small table in front of the
divan. A spirit lamp for the teapot. Pastries, fruits, and little
golden knives. And on the armchairs in affected, helpless
poses lie dolls—an old woman wearing a yellowish-red
sarafan; a fine fellow in a fiery peasant shirt who's got on a
velveteen sleeveless jacket and a round hat with peacock
feathers; a marquise in a white cotton wig; a harlequin;
Columbine . . .

"Well, sir, here I am."

She puts the teapot on the spirit lamp, lights the wick,
collects the toys from the armchairs, and smiles as she drops
them in my lap.

"My new *chefs-d'oeuvre*. Admire and criticize."

I admire. Trying to seem interested, attentive, and impar-
tial, I make up all kinds of trivial criticisms, interspersing
them with flattery. She pours tea—"Of course, you drink it
stronger, don't you?" With a smile, she hands me a cup with
her little finger pointed up. And a conversation begins, if
you could call it a conversation. She is usually the only one
who does any talking. About what? About this, that, and the
other. First about the toys, which I can't stand. Yet I keep
looking at them even during the conversation, since these
are "her passion, the only things she's given her soul to,
which she's created for art alone." Then she talks about her
husband, whom I've yet to see. She speaks of him with a
false gaiety ("He sleeps till ten, goes to work, eats dinner,
sleeps again, and leaves again!"). Finally, she talks about

her first child who died. She talks only about herself. She doesn't say a word about me, not even to be polite. Up to now, she knows nothing about me and hasn't shown the slightest intention of finding out who I am, what I am, where I work, if I'm married or single.

She's now especially excited, both excited and somehow very gay. She's talking incessantly, with unusual energy, demanding so much of my attention that I soon begin to lose my mind, grow stiff, and smile a foolish, confused smile. She suddenly jumps up—"Oh, I've forgotten the main thing I wanted to show you!"—disappears for an instant into the next room, and returns with a triumphant smile.

"*Voilà!* And I did it all by hand! Isn't it good?"

Her hands are holding something strange and terrible—a loose, full-length, sleeveless garment made of brown, unbleached linen, the kind peasants wear. She has sewn stripes and embroidery on the shoulders, armholes, bodice, and hem in dark-brown, indigo silk. She shows all of it to me, holding it up against her, against her full breasts and rounded stomach, then looks at me inquisitively, joyfully. I stand up and with feigned interest thoroughly examine it one more time. I pretend to admire it, but already can't bear to look at it. There is something somber, ancient, and somehow death-like in this sarafan. Something terrible and very unpleasant about it stirs within me thoughts associated with her pregnancy and tragic gaiety. Most likely, she is going to die in childbirth . . .

Tossing the sarafan onto the piano, she sits beside me. Looking intently at me, she begins to tell me her feelings for the unborn child. They are extraordinary, inexpressible. "With horror and ecstasy," she "feels within her a new being, and is already full of a love before which any other love, especially that for a man, is—blasphemy, vulgarity." If God takes this love away from her, she will commit suicide without giving it a second thought. She's already made up her mind about it . . . Or she'll run off to a convent . . . She's cherished the thought of entering a convent for the longest time now. Oh, if it weren't for marriage and children! She wouldn't hesitate for a moment! But even taking that into account, why should she hesitate, for whom should she hesitate? For what, for whom should she sacrifice herself?

"Tell me, my dear, for whom?" she passionately asks while staring at me. "Should it be for the man who scarcely knows I have a life of my own, that I have my own joys and sorrows which I share with no one in the whole wide world?"

Not looking away from me, she tries to laugh. You see, her husband is really not a normal person at all. There's something strange in the devoted way he always falls asleep whenever he's got the chance! First she leans back against the armchair, then she leans forward, putting her hands on mine. And I hear all her fragrances—the smell of her breathing, her hair, body, dress. Her cheeks are now ablaze, eyes really magnificent, movements sharp. Precious stones are sparkling on her breast, her fingers, her ears. While she's talking, I'm looking at her stomach, which is round beneath the velvet. I'm looking at the way she's shifting from one leg to the other, showing much of her loose, gray stocking . . .

Suddenly, realizing that the very minute has arrived, that the mysterious hope has come which brought me here, which has not vanished throughout this night, I take her hand and mumble, "Enough, my dear. Calm down!" I draw her to me. And she suddenly bites her lower lip, quickly puts a handkerchief to her lips, moves closer to me on the divan, and lays her tearful face on my chest . . .

I return at two in the morning. Not a soul is on the streets. The wind has changed, blowing stronger, with the smell of the sea. Stray raindrops fall in my face. The clouds above are no longer white. A thick blackness hangs over Moscow. And I hurriedly walk on.

"Run, run, it's already morning," the words keep going through my head. "To Kiev, to Warsaw, to the Crimea—wherever your eyes may roam!"

[1925]

An Endless Sunset

THE RAIN AT DUSK WAS making a heavy, monotonous noise in the garden near the house. That sweet freshness of wet vegetation in May was being drawn into the parlor through an open window. The sound of thunder rolled above the roof, grew louder as it rumbled, and burst with a crash when the reddish lightning flashed. And the sky grew dark with storm clouds hanging overhead.

Then the farm hands, in wet cloth jackets, rode in from the fields. Standing next to the barn, they began unharnessing the dirty plows, then herded the animals in, filling the entire estate with the sound of bellowing and bleating. The old women—tucking up the hems of their skirts—ran around the barnyard sparkling their bare white feet on the grass as they chased the sheep. A little shepherd wearing an enormous cap and tattered bast shoes chased a cow around the garden and fell headfirst into a clump of rain-drenched burdocks when it rushed noisily into a thicket. Night fell, the rain stopped. But my father, who had gone to the fields that morning, had not yet returned.

I was the only one at home. Back then, though, I was never bored. I still hadn't started really enjoying my role as housekeeper or the freedom I now had after graduating from the Gymnasium. My brother Pasha was studying at a military school. Anyuta, who had been married when Mama was still alive, was living in Kursk. My father and I were spending my first winter in the country by ourselves.

I was healthy and attractive, happy with myself, happy even by how easy it was for me to walk and run, to do anything around the house, to tell the servants what to do. While working, I would hum tunes I'd made up, tunes which deeply touched me. Looking at myself in the mirror, I couldn't keep from smiling. It seemed that anything I wore looked good, even though I dressed quite simply.

As soon as the rain had passed, I threw a shawl over my shoulders, snatched up the hem of my skirt, and ran to the trough where the old women were milking the cows. Several raindrops fell from the sky onto my bare head. But the thin, faint clouds high above the barnyard had already scattered, and a strange twilight—typical of our May nights—hovered above the yard. The freshness of wet grasses drifting in from the fields blended with a smoky smell coming from the servants' quarters. I even looked in there for a minute. The field hands—young peasant men wearing white chamois shirts—were sitting around a table drinking cups of soup. When I appeared, they stood up. I walked to the table. Smiling because I'd been running and was out of breath, I asked:

"Where's Papa? Was he still in the fields when you left?"

"He was there a short time, then drove off," several voices immediately replied.

"Drove off on what?"

"A *drozhky*, with young master Sievers."

"Is he really here?" I asked in a barely audible voice, struck by the news of this unexpected arrival. Yet catching myself in time, I just nodded and left slightly faster than I'd arrived.

Sievers had graduated from the Petrov Academy, and was

serving in the army. Even when I was a child, people had called me his fiancée, and he had disliked me intensely for this. But later, I often thought of him as my fiancé. Even before he had left in August to join up with his regiment, before he'd walked to our estate wearing his soldier's shirt with its shoulder straps, even before this enlisted man—with a pleasant look on his face—had told us the "folklore" of the Little Russian sergeant major, I was already getting used to the idea of becoming his wife. Gay, suntanned—only the upper half of his forehead was distinctly white—he was very dear to me.

"He must be on leave," I thought excitedly. I was pleased he had apparently come to see me. And uneasy. I rushed to the house to cook supper for my father, but when I entered the butler's quarters saw him already pacing the parlor, stomping his boots to the floor. And for some reason, he was especially glad to see me. His hat was pushed back, his beard tangled, his long boots and tussore jacket spattered with dirt. Yet in looking at him, I thought he was the personification of male strength and beauty.

"Why are you there in the dark?" I asked.

"Well, Tata," he replied, calling me by my childhood nickname, "I'm going to lie down now. I won't be eating supper. I'm exhausted. By the way, do you know what time it is? Now we'll have sunset all night long—sunset meets sunrise, as the peasants say. Maybe I could have some milk," he added absentmindedly.

I leaned over toward the lamp, and he began shaking his head. Looking at the glass in the light to be sure there weren't any flies in it, he started drinking the milk. By now, the nightingales were singing in the garden. And through those three windows facing the northwest, I could see the faraway, bright-green sky standing above the violet storm clouds of spring, clouds with a delicate, beautiful outline. Everything was hazy on the earth, in the sky. All the colors were softened by the faint dusk of the late night. I could see everything in the twilight of a sunset which would not die. I calmly answered my father's questions about the housework. But when he suddenly said that Sievers would be visiting us the next day, I could feel myself blush.

"Why?" I mumbled.

"To ask you to marry him," my father answered with a forced smile. "Why not? He's a handsome, smart fellow. He'll do a good job running his estate . . . We've already had plenty of drinks celebrating your marriage."

"Don't talk that way, Papa," I said, and tears came to my eyes.

My father looked at me for a long while. Then he kissed my forehead, and walked to the doors of his study.

"Morning is wiser than evening," he smiled.

II

Drowsy flies, perturbed by our conversation, were humming quietly on the ceiling. Gradually falling asleep, the clock began sputtering, then loudly, sadly cuckooed the hour of eleven . . .

"Morning is wiser than evening." My father's soothing words again came to mind. I was once more relaxed and happy in a sad sort of way.

My father was already asleep. The study had been quiet for a long time now. Everything on the estate was also sleeping. And there was something in the late-night silence following the rain, something blessed in the strained warbling of the nightingales. Something intangibly beautiful hovered above the sunset's distant twilight.

Trying not to make any noise, I got up quietly to clear the table. Tiptoeing from the room, I put the milk, honey, and meat in the cold stove in the front hallway. I covered the tea service, and went to my room. But I wasn't shut off from the nightingales and sunset. The shutters of my window were closed, but I could see the twilight in the living room by looking through the open door which connected both rooms.

I could hear the singing of nightingales throughout the house. Letting my hair down around my shoulders, I sat for a long time on my bed trying to decide something. Then I shut my eyes, leaned my head back on the pillow, and instantly fell asleep. Right above me, someone said in a distinct voice, "Sievers!" It startled me, and I awoke. Suddenly, the thought of marriage ran through my body with a sweet horror, a chill . . .

I lay there a long time as if half-conscious, not thinking about anything. Then I imagined being all alone at the estate, being already married, imagined that on a night such as this my husband was returning from town, that he'd walked into the house and was quietly taking off his overcoat in the front hallway, that I was waiting for him—that he just as quietly appeared in the doorway of my bedroom . . . How joyfully he lifted me in his arms! And I began to feel as if I really were in love.

I didn't know Sievers well. The man with whom I spent this most tender night of my first love didn't look like Sievers, but it seemed to me that Sievers was the one I was thinking of. I hadn't seen him for nearly a year, and the night made him seem better looking, more desirable. It was quiet, dark. I lay there and suddenly felt I was no longer in the real world. "Why not? He's handsome, smart . . . " And smiling, I looked into that darkness of closed eyes where indistinct faces and patches of light were drifting . . .

At the same time, I felt that the darkest hour of the night had come. "If Masha were home," I thought as my mind turned to the maid, "I'd go to her room right now and talk with her until dawn . . . But no," I thought again, "it's better alone. I'll confide in her when I'm married . . . "

Something cracked timidly in the living room. I listened carefully, then opened my eyes. It had grown darker in there. Everything around me, everything within me had already changed. It was a different life now, a special late-night life which would be difficult to understand in the morning. The nightingales were silent now. Only one—the nightingale which had built a nest this spring by the balcony—was warbling, warbling slowly. The pendulum in the living room was ticking carefully, in exact time. In some way, the silence of the house seemed full of tension.

Listening carefully to every rustle, I sat up in bed with the feeling that I was in complete control of this mysterious hour, one made for kisses, for stolen embraces. And the most improbable things I could imagine, the most improbable expectations seemed entirely possible. I suddenly remembered how Sievers had jokingly promised to come sometime late at night to meet me in our garden . . . But what if he weren't joking? What if he were slowly, silently strolling onto the balcony right now?

Leaning my head back onto the pillow, I stared at the quivering twilight. And as I imagined opening the balcony door, I thought of everything I would faintly whisper to him as I sweetly lost control of myself, as I let him take me along the moist sands of the tree-lined path into the depths of the wet garden . . .

III

I put on my shoes, threw a shawl over my shoulders, carefully walked into the living room, and stopped with a pounding heart at the balcony door. Convinced that only the steady ticking of the clock and the echoing nightingale could be heard in the house, I turned the key in the lock without making a sound. Right away, the nightingale's warbling—reverberating throughout the garden—grew louder. The tense stillness vanished, and I breathed the night's fragrant dampness with a feeling of freedom.

In the sun's twilight—darkened by storm clouds in the north—I walked along the wet sand of a long path lined

76

with young birches. I walked to the end of the garden, where a lilac-covered gazebo stood surrounded by poplars and aspens. It was so quiet there that I could hear occasional drops of water falling from the hanging branches. Everything was dozing, seemingly delighted in its drowsiness. Only the nightingale yearned as it sang sweetly. My heart skipped—every shadow was like a human figure. And when at last I walked into the gazebo and smelled its warmth on me, I was almost certain that someone had just then silently held me closely in his arms.

Yet no one was there. And I stood trembling with excitement, carefully listening to the high-pitched, sleepy babble of aspens. I then sat down on the damp bench . . . I was still waiting for something, at times glancing at the breaking dawn. More and more, I felt an intimate, indescribable happiness blowing all around me. It was that great, terrible happiness which all of us eventually encounter at the crossroads of life. It suddenly touched me, perhaps doing precisely what it was supposed to do—touch, then go away. All those tender words deep in my heart finally brought tears to my eyes. Leaning against the trunk of a damp poplar, I suddenly heard the sound, the soothing sound, of babbling leaves growing faintly louder, then dying. And I was happy as I wept silent tears.

I observed the night being secretly transformed into dawn. I saw the twilight grow pale, and through a distant cherry orchard watched a little white cloud in the north turn scarlet. The air became cooler. I wrapped myself in the shawl. And in the sky's brightening expanse, which looked ever larger, ever deeper, Venus quivered through a pure, bright drop of water. I loved someone, and my love was in everything—in the cold, in the aroma of the morning, the freshness of the lush garden, the morning star . . .

But then I heard the pump's sharp screech as it passed the garden out onto the river. Then someone cried out in the barnyard in a hoarse, morning voice. I slipped from the gazebo, hurried to the balcony, opened the door gently, quietly, and ran on tiptoes into the warm darkness of my bedroom.

In the morning, Sievers was shooting jackdaws in our garden. It was like a shepherd walking into the house banging a large knout. But this didn't stop me from sleeping. When I finally awoke, voices were ringing out, plates clattering in the dining room. Then Sievers came to my door and shouted:

"Natalya Alexeyevna! Shame on you! You've overslept!"

And I really should have been ashamed, ashamed to see him, ashamed for refusing to marry him—now I was sure of it. Rushing to get dressed, glancing now and then in the mirror at my pale face, I shouted a joking, friendly reply. Yet I shouted it so faintly that he probably didn't hear me.

[1903-1926]

A Mask

A WINTER EVENING AT THE Nikolayev Station in Petersburg. The trains are leaving for Moscow. The station's snack bar is noisy and crowded. Everyone's in too great a hurry to eat and drink. All are wearing cumbersome, hot traveling clothes. Round-headed Tartar waiters dash madly, carrying plates of food. The air is thick, pungent, hot . . .

With a look of absolute calm, she's sitting at the next table. I'm eating, and glance at her now and then. She's pretending to be absorbed in a newspaper. She's ordered veal, then bought *The New Times,* and—with arched eyebrows—is reading it, though anyone can plainly see that she doesn't understand a single word. A newspaper isn't her style. She's not used to one and really doesn't want it. She strongly senses my presence, my veiled curiosity. Misinterpreting it, she's waiting for me just about now to turn to her and ask something like:

"I'm sorry, but are you also going to Moscow, or are you waiting for the Vologda train?"

But I say nothing, glance at her, and eat. Yet she's already getting nervous, arches her eyebrows even higher, and all the more anxiously leafs through the pages of the news-

79

paper as if searching for something important. Finally, she can't stand it any longer.

"Pardon me," she asks coldly, in a tone of sadness. "You don't know, do you, if there's been any news from the Front in this evening's papers? I'm terribly worried about my husband. I haven't received a letter from him in three months... He's a pilot—insanely brave..."

"I haven't seen the evening papers. I can't tell you."

"A pity," she says—more coldly this time—raises her eyebrows, and once more buries herself in the paper. She's wearing a blue, long-waisted man's jacket over a dress of white wool. A white Caucasian cap. Her eyes—far from young—are outlined with thick, dark-blue make-up. Broad cheekbones powdered as if whitewashed. Fingers big and strong flashing sharp, long, almond-colored nails. A heavy scent, like that of a dog...

And then suddenly, looking hopelessly for somewhere to sit, a young officer with a red moustache approaches the little table. He's wearing a new greatcoat made of military cloth. Shining shoulder straps. He's blushing, touching the brim of his hat, clicking his heels, and timidly sitting on the chair opposite her.

"Do you mind?"

Within five minutes, he's brought her Sauterne. She's riveted her attention on the veal, handling her knife and fork with dexterity, with her little finger pointed in an affected manner. Raised eyebrows, a sad smile. He's blushing all over, getting up his courage, unbuttoning his coat, smoking, talking nonstop. She keeps shrugging her shoulders, carefully giving brief replies to his phony arguments that life is "beautiful all the same." She repeats the same, enigmatic phrases:

"It depends on the person..."

"It's a matter of taste..."

"Life can't be kept within narrow bounds..."

He passionately objects:

"Oh, you're so terribly skeptical! On the surface, you seem to be so cheerful, so energetic, whereas . . . "

She lightly taps her knife against the plate, and with an absentminded sadness asks a waiter, "Gimme a cup of black cafe," then says with a sigh:

"No, you're bitterly mistaken. My heart is full of mourning. My husband is also an officer, an artilleryman. And I've just received the awful news that he's been fatally wounded . . . I just know how to wear a mask extremely well!"

[1930]

The Murderess

A HOUSE WITH A MEZZANINE in the Zamoskvorechya. Wooden. Clean windows. Decorated with a good, bluish paint. In front, a crowd and large government automobile. Through the open front doors, gray carpeting ascending the staircase with a strip of red stair-carpet running up the middle. A whole crowd looking in there with delight, and the sound of a melodious voice:

"Yes, my dears, she killed 'im! Young widow she was, come from a rich family . . . They say she was crazy in love with him. But he liked her only for her money, then got to fooling around with somebody else. So she invites 'im to her place to say goodbye, feeds 'im, gives 'im some wine, and all the while keeps repeatin', 'Let me feast my eyes on you!' And then she seats 'im—tipsy he is—and stabs 'im right in the heart . . . "

Someone opens the mezzanine window. A white-gloved hand signals to the automobile. The car's engine begins to sound, the crowd makes way. And then she appears. First her slender legs, then the flaps of her sable jacket, and then all of her, so well-dressed. Treading lightly as if going to the church on her wedding day, she starts walking down the stairs. White and plump, black eyes and black eyebrows, the uncovered head, smoothly combed hair parted in the middle, long earrings sparkling, bobbing on her ears. A tranquil, lucid face, an affectionate smile for the crowd . . .

She enters the car, sits down, the authorities get in after her, a man wearing an uncomfortable overcoat looks sternly, with dissatisfaction, at the curious onlookers. The door slams shut, the car instantly pulls away . . .

And the crowd gazes with admiration:

"Gee, they took 'em for a drive, took 'em away!"

[1930]

First Love

$\mathcal{S}$UMMER. AN ESTATE IN
a forested western region. All day long, a fresh, pouring
rain, its continual sound on the plank roof. In the hushed
house, twilight, boredom, flies sleeping on the ceiling. In
the garden, wet trees drooping submissively under the
water's rushing net. Red flower beds—unusually bright—on
the balcony. Above the garden, in the hazy sky, a stork
appears distinctly, anxiously. Thin and black, crestfallen,
with tail tucked under, it's been standing at the edge of its
nest on the top of an ancient birch tree, standing in the
ruins of the tree's bare, white twigs. Indignant at times, it
gets excited, jumps up and down, taps its beak with a sharp
wooden sound:

"What's this? A flood, a real flood!"

It's about four o'clock. The rain is brighter and is subsid-
ing. Someone lights the samovar in the front hallway—the
smoke's balmy scent spreads all over the estate.

By sunset, all is clean, silent, tranquil. The owners of the
manor and their guests go for a walk in the pine forest.

The evening sky has already turned blue. The roads are
moist and spongy in the forest clearings covered with yellow
needles. The forest is fragrant, damp, and resonant—some-

one's distant voice, prolonged call, or echo reverberates in an astonishing way in the farthest thickets. The clearings seem narrow. Their neat, endless corridors vanish in the evening distance. The forest walls lining them are majestically immense, crowded in the darkness. At the top, their masts are bare, smooth, red. Farther down, they are gray, rough, mossy, then collide with each other. Moss, lichens, rotten twigs, and something else drooping like the greenish, dishevelled hair of fairy-tale forest monsters form jungles, a kind of primeval Russia. And as you walk out into the clearing, the sight of a pine sprig fills you with a feeling of happiness. It is pale-white, a delicate marsh-green, not heavy, yet strong and branchy. In the spray and watery dust, it stands there as if under a blanket of spangled, silver muslin.

That night, a young cadet was out walking with a big, friendly dog. They were running ahead of the others, continually playing, chasing each other. Alongside them, a teenage girl was walking demurely, gracefully. She had long arms and legs, and was wearing a little checkered overcoat which for some reason seemed quite nice. And everyone else was grinning, knowing why the young cadet was running so, why he was playing so feverishly, why he was pretending to be having so much fun—why he was ready to start weeping in despair.

The girl also knew why, and was proud, contented. Yet she casually looked at everything in disgust.

[1930]

A Hunchback's Romance

THE HUNCHBACK HAD received an anonymous love letter inviting him to a rendezvous:

> On Saturday, April 5th, meet me on Cathedral Square at seven in the evening. I'm young, rich, single, and—why hide it?—I've love your proud, sorrowful gaze, your noble, intelligent brow, your solitary manner . . . I want only to hope that you too will perhaps find a kindred spirit in me . . . You will recognize me by my gray, English dress. I'll be carrying a violet, silk parasol in my left hand, a small bouquet of violets in my right . . .

How he was staggered by the note—the first love letter he'd received in his entire life. How he awaited Saturday! When it arrived, he went to the barbershop, then bought new (lilac-colored) gloves and a new tie—with a flash of gray to match his suit. At home in front of the mirror, he repeatedly re-tied this tie with his cold and trembling, long, thin fingers. A red, splotchy blush spread beneath the delicate skin of his cheeks. His beautiful eyes grew dark . . .

Later, he sat all dressed up in an armchair, like a guest, as

86

if he were a stranger   visiting his own apartment. And he began waiting for the fatal hour. At last, the clock in the dining room struck half past six with a terrible, penetrating ring, a ring of great significance. He shuddered, got up, tried to restrain himself as he put on his summer hat in the front hallway, took his cane—and slowly left. Yet on the street, he could control himself no longer. His long, thin legs walked faster and faster. He walked with all the defiant importance his hump gave him. Yet he was seized by that blessed fear of impending happiness.

Then he rushed onto the square, rushed toward the cathedral, and suddenly froze. Walking straight toward him in the pink sunset, striding with an air of importance, wearing a gray dress and nice hat looking like something a man would wear, carrying a parasol in her left hand and violets in her right was—a hunchbacked woman.

Someone had played a merciless trick on the man!

[1930]

The Man-Eater

A DESTITUTE GIRL. AN orphan. Ugly in a pretty sort of way. Extremely quiet. Almost a little fool. Hired on at a nobleman's estate. Given dirty, hard work—unquestioningly, mutely exhausting herself as she tried to please in every way possible. The overseer, the oldest man working on the estate, a retired grenadier, quickly corrupted her innocence—she submitted after resisting in a despairing, pitiful, childlike way.

A month later, she was pregnant. Everyone knew all about it. The overseer's wife raised hell, and the lady of the manor hastily fired the girl. With tears all over her face, the girl somehow shoved the few possessions she had into a bag and ran out of the courtyard. The overseer's wife, standing in the doorway of the servants' quarters, wildly rejoiced— wobbling, whistling, turning the dogs loose on the girl, beating a bone against a copper basin, and crying in different pitches:

"Bitch! Beggar! Tramp! Man-eater! Witch!"

[1931]

The Caucasus

AFTER ARRIVING IN MOSCOW, I lived like a thief in a hotel hidden away on a narrow street near the Arbat. I lived there in agony, like a hermit—waiting for my next rendezvous with her. She came to see me three times while I was staying there. And each time, she would rush into the room and say:

"I can only be a minute . . . "

She was pale with the beautiful paleness of a woman passionately in love. Her words burst forth, she tossed her parasol wherever it might fall, hastily lifted her veil, and embraced me. I was moved by her pity, her delirious joy.

"I've got a feeling he's suspecting something, that he might even know something," she said. "Maybe he's read one of your letters, gotten his hands on the key to my desk . . . A man with the cruel, conceited character he's got is capable of just about anything. He once told me bluntly, 'Nothing would stop me from defending my honor, the honor of a husband and officer!' Now he's watching literally every step I take! If our plan's going to succeed, I've got to be awfully careful. He's already agreed to let me go, since I hinted I would die if I didn't see the South, the sea. But for God's sake, please be patient!"

Ours was a bold plan—to leave on the same train for the Caucasian coast, then live there for three to four weeks in the wild. I knew the coastline, for I'd lived near Sochi when I was young and by myself. Ever since then, I'd remembered those autumn evenings surrounded by black cypresses near the cold, gray waves . . . And she grew pale when I said, "And now I'll be there with you, in the mountain jungles, by the tropical sea . . ." Until the last moment, we didn't believe our plan would work—it seemed too great a happiness.

Cold rains were falling on Moscow. Summer already appeared to have gone, not to return. The weather was dirty, gloomy. The streets were wet, sparkling black with the opened umbrellas of pedestrians and the upraised tops of the horse-drawn taxis that shook as they moved. And the wind was dark and loathsome when I went to the train station. The anxiety and coldness made everything within me freeze. I ran between the station and platform pulling my hat toward my eyes, burying my face in the collar of my overcoat.

In my small, first-class compartment, I could hear rain pouring on the roof. I quickly lowered the curtain. As soon as the porter had wiped his wet hand on his white apron, taken my order for tea, and left, I locked the door. Then I barely moved the curtain aside and stood absolutely still, all the while watching the diverse crowd of people scurrying back and forth with their things in front of the railway car in the dim light of the station lamps.

We had agreed that I would come to the station as early as possible. She would arrive as late as possible so that I would not run into both of them on the platform. They should have been here by now. I strained my eyes even more—they still hadn't come. The second bell rang—I grew cold with fear. She was late, or at the last minute he'd refused to let her go! Yet suddenly, I was struck by the sight of his tall figure, his officer's hat, narrow greatcoat, and hand in a suede glove wrapped around her arm as he strode toward the car.

I stepped back from the window and collapsed onto a corner of the divan. A second-class coach was next to mine. I imagined him confidently boarding it with her, looking around—had the porter fixed everything just right?—taking off his glove, his hat, kissing her, making the sign of the cross over her . . . The third bell made a deafening sound. As the train began pulling out of the station, it plunged into numbness. It moved away, shaking, bouncing, then began riding smoothly as it picked up speed. With an ice-cold hand, I thrust a ten-ruble bill into the hand of the conductor who had brought her to my compartment, who had carried her things from the other coach . . .

She didn't even kiss me as she walked in, only smiled with a look of pity, sat down on the divan, and unsnagged her hat from her hair as she took it off.

"I couldn't eat a bite," she said. "I thought I couldn't go on playing this awful role to the end. I'm dying for something to drink. Give me some Narzan," she said, for the first time addressing me with the familiar form of "you." "I'm certain he's going to follow me. I gave him two addresses— Gelendzhik and Gagra. In about three or four days, he'll be in Gelendzhik . . . Yet God be with him. Death would be better than being tormented this way . . . "

The corridor was sunny and stifling when I walked into it the following morning. The odor of soap, cologne, and all the morning smells of a passenger coach were coming from the washrooms. On the other side of the warmed, dust-clouded windows, the flat, scorched earth was passing by. I could see wide, dusty roads and ox-drawn carts. Railway booths with front gardens filled with canary-yellow rings of sunflowers and scarlet hollyhocks suddenly appeared. And it went on—the infinite expanse of bare plains marked with burial mounds and sepulchres. The unbearable, dry sun. The sky which looked like a dusty storm cloud. Then signs on the horizon of the first mountains . . .

■

She sent him a postcard from Gelendzhik and Gagra. She wrote that she still didn't know where she would be staying.

We got off the train while traveling south along the coastline.

We found a forest primeval, overgrown with plane trees, flowering shrubs, redwood, magnolias, pomegranates from which fan-like palms emerged. The cypresses grew black . . .

I would wake up early in the morning. She would sleep until it was time for tea, which we drank at about seven. While she was sleeping, I'd walk along the hills into the thickets. The sun here—hotter than in the north—was already strong, clean, and joyful. In the forest, the fragrant mist shone with the color of azure, separated, and melted. The perpetual whiteness of the snowy mountains beamed beyond the faraway tops of the forest.

I would return by way of our scorching country market-place, which smelled of chimneys burning manure. Business was brisk. The marketplace was crowded with people, with saddled horses, and small donkeys. Mountaineers of many tribes gathered there in the mornings. Circassian women glided over the ground in long black clothes which touched the earth. They wore red Caucasian slippers. Their heads were wrapped in something black, their glances quick, flashing at times from within this funereal, veiled headdress.

Later, we would walk to the seashore, which was always abandoned. We swam and lay in the sun until lunch. After we'd eaten—fish fried on a grill, white wine, nuts and fruit—hot, gay strips of light would stretch through the partially closed shutters into the twilight of our tile-roofed hut.

When the heat subsided and we opened the window, we could see a patch of sea between the cypresses standing on a cliff below us. That patch was the color of violets, and lay so smoothly, so peacefully, that we thought there would be no end to this tranquility, this beauty.

At sunset, wondrous clouds beyond the sea often piled on top of each other. They drifted in such a magnificent way that sometimes she lay on the ottoman, covered her face with a transparent scarf, and wept—in two or three weeks, it would be back to Moscow!

The nights were warm, pitch-black. Fireflies floated in the darkness, twinkling, shining with the glow of topaz. The wood frogs sounded like the ringing of little glass bells. When our eyes got used to the darkness, stars and mountain ridges would ascend into the sky. Trees we hadn't noticed in the day appeared above the countryside. And all night long, we could hear from over there, from the Caucasian tavern, the hollow beating of a drum and the throaty, mournful, hopelessly happy yelling of what seemed to be the same endless song.

Not far from us, in a ravine near the seashore, a small, clear brook jetted along its stony bed as it rushed from the forest to the sea. How marvelously its sparkle disintegrated and boiled at that mysterious hour when the late-night moon—like some kind of wonderful creature—came from behind the mountains, the forests—and stared!

Threatening thunderclouds sometimes drifted down from the mountains. A wicked storm would move in. Enchanted chasms of green would gape from time to time in the noisy, deathly forest blackness. And antediluvian claps of thunder would split the celestial heights. It was then that eaglets would wake up in the forest and caterwaul. The snow leopard would roar, the jackals yelp... A whole pack of them once clustered in the light of our window—on nights like this, they always gather near human dwellings. We opened the window and looked down at them. They were standing in the glittering downpour yapping, begging for help. She wept with joy while looking at them.

■

He searched for her in Gelendzhik, Gagra, and Sochi. The morning after arriving in Sochi, he swam in the sea, then shaved, put on clean underwear, a snow-white tunic, had breakfast on the restaurant terrace of his hotel, drank a bottle of champagne, drank coffee with Chartreuse, and slowly smoked a cigar down to its end. Returning to his hotel room, he lay on the divan and shot himself in the temples with two revolvers.

[1937]

Muza

ALTHOUGH NO LONGER a young man by then, I had decided to take up painting. I'd always had a passionate interest in it. Leaving my estate in Tambov province, I spent the winter in Moscow taking lessons from an artist who lacked talent, yet was rather well-known. He was sloppy, fat, and had picked up the usual habits—long hair with great big greasy curls combed back, a pipe in his teeth, a rich red velvet jacket, dirt-gray spats—I especially hated them—an off-handed manner of talking, a condescending way of narrowing his eyes when he glanced at a student's work while saying to himself:

"Amusing, very amusing . . . Undoubted successes . . . "

I was living in the Arbat in the Capital Hotel, right next to the Prague Restaurant. During the days, I would work at the artist's place or in my hotel room. I'd frequently spend evenings in cheap restaurants with various bohemian acquaintances I'd just met. They were young and ragged, devoted to billiards and beer served with crayfish. I lived a boring, unpleasant life—this effeminate, slovenly artist, his studio "artistically" cluttered, full of all sorts of dusty props. This gloomy Capital Hotel! I can recall the snow falling incessantly outside the windows, the horse-drawn trolleys sounding with a muffled rattle in the Arbat, evenings in the dimly lit restaurant that reeked with the sour stink of beer and gaslights. I don't understand why I led such a wretched existence—at the time, I was far from poor.

And then one March, I was sitting in my hotel room drawing with crayons. Rain and the wet dampness of what was no longer a winter snow were coming in through my open double-windows. The horses' hooves weren't clattering along the bridges as they do in winter. The trolleys were making a sort of musical sound. And then someone knocked at my door.

"Who's there?" I shouted. But there was no reply. I waited, and shouted once more. Again, there was silence, then another knock. I got up and opened the door. A tall young woman was standing there. She was wearing a small gray winter hat, a straight gray overcoat, and gray boots. With eyes the color of acorns, she was staring from under her long eyelashes. Raindrops sparkled on her hair and under the brim of her hat. She stared and said:

"I am Muza Graf, a student at the Conservatory. I heard you were an interesting person and came to meet you. Do you have any objections?"

A little surprised, I of course politely answered:

"I'm very flattered. Welcome. Only I must warn you that what you've heard about me is hardly true. I'm not a very interesting person."

"In any case, let me come in. Don't keep me standing out here in the hallway," she said, staring at me even more. "Be flattered if you like, but ask me in."

And walking into the room, she made herself at home, took off her hat in front of my mirror of gray-silver which had turned black in places. She straightened her chestnut hair, threw off her coat and tossed it onto a chair, stood there in a checked flannel dress, sat on the divan, sniffed with a nose wet from the rain and snow, and issued the command:

"Take off my boots and hand me the handkerchief that's in my coat pocket."

I gave her the handkerchief, she wiped her nose, then stretched her legs toward me:

"I saw you last night at the Shor concert," she said indifferently.

Trying to hold back a stupid smile of satisfaction and disbelief—what an odd visitor!—I dutifully took one boot off, then the other. She still smelled of fresh air, and this aroma excited me. I was excited by that masculinity of hers that was fused to her feminine youthfulness, by the look on her face, the staring eyes, the strong, beautiful hand. I was excited by all I saw and sensed while taking the boots off from under her dress. I saw her rounded, strong knees lying beneath the dress, her prominent calves in thin, gray stockings, and the pointed feet in their patent-leather slippers.

Then she settled comfortably on the divan, apparently preparing to stay for some time. Not knowing what to say, I began asking her who had told her about me, what she had heard, who she was, where she lived, and with whom. She replied:

"Who told me and what I heard is not important. I came here primarily because I saw you at the concert. You're not bad looking. I'm a doctor's daughter, and live not far from here on Prechistensky Boulevard."

She spoke with a certain suddenness, terseness. Again not knowing what to say, I asked:

"Do you want some tea?"

"I do," she said, "and if you've got the money, send out for some rennet apples at Belov's. It's right here in the Arbat. Only have the bellboy make it snappy—I'm impatient."

"Yet you seem so calm."

"Things are seldom what they seem . . . "

After the bellboy brought a samovar and little sack of apples, she brewed the tea and wiped the cups and spoons, both of which were already clean. Having eaten an apple and finished a cup of tea, she settled deeper into the divan and clapped her hand several times up and down on the divan's empty seat:

"Now sit close to me."

I sat down. She embraced me and slowly kissed my lips. She sat back, looked at me as if convincing herself I deserved this, closed her eyes, and kissed me again—a long, passionate kiss.

"Well, then," she said as if relieved. "No more for now. The day after tomorrow."

The hotel room was already totally dark—we could see only the sad faintness of the street lights. It's easy to imagine what I was feeling. Where had happiness like this suddenly come from? Young, strong, extraordinary style and shape of lips . . . As if in a dream, I heard the monotonous sound of the trolleys, the clatter of hooves . . .

"The day after tomorrow, I want to have dinner with you at the Prague," she said. "I've never been there. I'm not very experienced. I can only imagine what you must be thinking of me. You're really my first love."

"Love?"

"What else would you call it?"

Of course, I soon gave up my art lessons. She continued hers somehow or other. The two of us were inseparable. We lived like newlyweds, visited the galleries, exhibitions, attended concerts and for some reason went to public lectures. In May, I moved at her request to a very old estate south of Moscow where small dachas had been built and were being rented out. She began coming down on the train to see me, and would return to Moscow at one in the morning. I'd never expected anything like this—dachas south of Moscow. I'd never lived the dacha life, with nothing to do, on an estate so unlike our estates in the steppes. I'd never lived in that kind of climate.

It rained the whole time. I was surrounded by forests of

pine. White clouds were always accumulating in the bright blue sky. High up, the thunder rolled. Then a sparkling rain would begin sprinkling in the sunlight and suddenly change from a sultry moistness into the fragrant steam of pines. Everything was wet, lush, like a mirror.

In the park on the grounds of the estate, the trees were so large that the dachas—I don't know how they'd been built there—seemed small. They seemed like those dwellings built beneath trees in tropical countries. The pond looked like a huge, black mirror, half of it jammed with duckweed. I lived at the edge of the park, in the forest. My log dacha was not completely finished. The walls were not yet caulked, the floors uneven, the stoves had no doors, and there was almost no furniture. And because of the perpetual dampness, a velvet mould grew all over my boots which I'd thrown under the bed.

The evenings would get dark only around midnight—the western twilight kept standing in the motionless, peaceful woods. On moonlit nights, it would mingle strangely with the moonlight, also motionless and bewitched. And judging by the peacefulness which reigned all around me, judging by the clearness of the sky and air, I would think the rain had passed. But then I'd fall asleep as I was riding with her to the railway station and suddenly hear a cloudburst accompanied by peals of thunder once more pouring on the roof. Darkness would surround us and lightning strike the ground at an angle.

In the morning, the shadows and blinding patches of sunlight would appear in so many different colors on the violet surface of the damp paths lined with trees. The small birds called flycatchers made a clicking sound, the thrushes chirped hoarsely. By noon, the air was again steamy, clouds moved in, and it started to sprinkle. Before dusk, the air became clear—a golden, crystal-like grid of light from the setting sun shone through a leaf into the windows and quivered against my timber walls.

Then I'd walk to the station to meet her. The train would pull in and countless dacha residents stream out onto the platform. I could smell the locomotive's coal and the damp freshness of the forest. She would appear in the crowd carrying a string bag loaded with packages of snacks, fruits, and a bottle of Madeira. Looking into each other's eyes, we would quickly eat dinner . . . Before her late-night departure, we'd wander through the park. She'd become a sleep-walker, walking as she leaned her head on my shoulder . . . The black pond, the ancient trees going off into the starry sky. The early morning with its infinite silence, with a bewitched light. And trees casting their endlessly long shadows onto silvery clearings resembling lakes.

In June, she came to my own place in the country. Although we weren't married, she lived with me as if she were my wife—she began supervising the housekeeping. She avoided boredom that long autumn by spending her time reading and doing daily chores. Of our neighbors, a man by the name of Zavistovsky visited us the most. He was an impoverished landowner who lived by himself about two versts from us. He was puny, with reddish hair, timid, not very bright, but not a bad musician. In the winter, he began dropping by almost every evening. I'd known him since childhood, and had by now become so used to him than an evening without him seemed strange. The two of us would play checkers, or he and Muza would play duets on the piano.

On a day sometime before Christmas, I drove to town, and returned after the moon had come up. Walking into the house, I couldn't find her anywhere, and sat alone at the samovar.

"But where's the lady, Dunya? Has she gone for a walk?"

"I don't know, milord. They haven't been home since lunch. They put their things on and left," my old nanny said gloomily, not looking up, as she walked through the dining room.

"She must have gone to Zavistovsky's," I thought. "Both of them will probably be here soon. It's already seven . . . " And I walked into the study, lay down, and immediately fell asleep—I was frozen from being on the road all day. And then an hour later I woke up just as suddenly with the clear, savage thought:

"She's left me! She's hired some peasant in the village to drive her to the station, then gone to Moscow. I wouldn't put anything past her! But is it possible she's come back?"

I walked through the house. No, she hadn't returned. I was ashamed the servants knew . . .

At about ten, not knowing what to do, I put on my sheepskin coat, for some reason took my rifle, and walked along the highway to Zavistovsky's, all the while thinking, "It's as if he purposely didn't come today. And I've still got to get through a terrible night! Has she really gone away, has she really left me? Of course not. It just couldn't be!" I crunched along the well-worn path leading through the snow. At my left, snowy fields shone beneath a low, miserable moon.

I turned off the highway and walked to the pitiful Zavistovsky estate on a path lined with barren trees leading through a field. I passed through the courtyard entrance, the old ramshackle house to the left. Darkness in the house . . . I walked up onto the iced porch and tugged open the heavy door covered on the inside with ragged upholstering. A stove with an open door was burning red in the front hallway. The room was warm and dark . . . But it was dark even in the parlor.

"Vikenty Vikentich!"

He appeared without making a sound. Wearing felt boots. Visible in the doorway of the study in only the moonlight pouring in through a triple-window.

"Ah, it's you . . . Come in, come in, please do . . . As you can see, I'm sitting here in the dark, in the moonlight, whiling away the night . . . "

I entered and sat down on a lumpy divan.

"Can you imagine? Muza's vanished somewhere . . . "

He was silent for a long time, then said in almost a whisper:

"Yes, yes, I understand . . . "

"What do you mean you understand?"

And just then, just as noiselessly, also wearing felt boots, with a shawl over her shoulders, Muza came out—out of the bedroom next to the study.

"You've got a rifle. If you want to shoot somebody, don't shoot him. Shoot me."

And she sat on the divan opposite me.

I looked at her boots, at the knees underneath the gray skirt. I could see everything quite well in the golden light coming down through the window. I wanted to shout, "I can't live without you! I'm ready to give up my life for these knees alone, for this skirt, these boots!"

"It's obvious the affair is over," she said. "There's no need to make a scene."

"You are monstrously cruel," I choked.

"Give me a cigarette," she said to Zavistovsky.

He leaned over in a cowardly way, strained as he reached his cigarette case to her and rummaged through his pockets for matches.

"You're already talking to me as if we were strangers," I said, gasping for air. "You could at least not be so intimate with him when I'm here."

"Why not?" she asked, raising her eyebrows, holding a cigarette in her outstretched hand.

My heart was already pounding in my throat, beating at my temples. I got up and staggered out the door.

[1938]

Emerald

THE BLUE, LATE-NIGHT blackness of the sky. White clouds drifting gently everywhere. Near the moon, up high, the clouds are a pale blue. But the more you look, it's not the clouds drifting, but the moon itself. A star's golden tear is flowing near it, flowing along with it. The moon is floating off into infinite heights, carrying the star higher and higher.

She's sitting sideways on the sill of an open window. With her head tilted back, she's looking up. The moving sky is making her a little dizzy. He's standing by her knees.

"What's that color? I can't decide! Can you, Tolya?"

"The color of what, Kisa?"

"Don't call me that. I've already told you a thousand times . . . "

"Yes, m'am, Kseniya Andreyevna."

"I'm talking about this sky in the clouds. What a wonderful color! Both frightening and wonderful! It's true—it really is celestial. There just aren't colors like that on earth. It's kind of emerald."

"Once it's in the sky, then of course it's celestial. But why emerald? I've never seen one in my whole life. You just like that word."

"Yes, well, I don't know. Maybe not emerald, maybe ruby . . . Only it's a color which you'd probably find only in heaven. When you look at all this, how can you not believe that there's a heaven, angels, the kingdom of God . . . "

"And golden pears on a willow tree . . . "

"You're such a degenerate, Tolya. Marya Sergeyevna is right when she says that the worst girl is still better than any young man."

"Her lips verbalize truth itself, Kisa."

Her dress is cotton, checkered. Cheap shoes. Plump, girlish calves and knees. A round little head with a small braid encircling it folded in back. He puts one hand on her knee, embraces her around the shoulders with the other arm, and half-jokingly kisses her slightly parted lips. She silently frees herself, taking his hand from her knee.

"What's the deal? Were we offended?"

She leans her head back against the window jamb. And he sees that she's crying.

"Well, what's the matter?"

"Oh, leave me alone . . . "

"Well, what happened?"

She whispers:

"Nothing . . . "

And jumping from the windowsill, she runs off.

He shrugs his shoulders:

"Foolish as a saint!"

[1940]

Rusya

AT ELEVEN O'CLOCK AT night, the Moscow-Sevastopol Express made an unscheduled stop at a little station on the other side of Podolsk. It waited there for something to arrive on the other track. In one of the first-class coaches, a gentleman and lady moved to a lowered window. As a conductor was crossing the tracks swinging a red lantern in his hand, the lady asked him:

"Tell me, why are we stopping here?"

The conductor replied that the mail train was late.

It was dark and melancholy at the station. The sun had long since gone down, yet in the west,beyond the station, beyond the blackening wooded fields, the lingering sunset of a Moscow summer was still shining with a deathly light. The damp smell of marshes came into the coach through the window. In the stillness, the passengers could hear the monotonous screaking of a corncrake coming from somewhere, a sound which also seemed permeated with dampness.

He leaned his elbows on the window, she leaned against his shoulder.

"I once spent a vacation near here," he said. "I was a tutor on a dacha estate about five *versts* from this station. It was a boring place. A sparse forest, magpies, mosquitoes, and dragonflies. The only place you could get a decent view was in the house itself, on the mezzanine, where you could clearly see the horizon. Of course, the house was built in the Russian style. It had been terribly neglected—the owners had lost most of their money. Something resembling a garden stood behind the house. Behind the garden was an area that was not quite a lake, not quite a marsh, overgrown with tall grasses and water lilies. And just as you would expect, a flat-bottomed boat was tied along the swampy shore.''

"And, of course, there was a bored young dacha miss whom you rowed around the marsh.''

"Yes, everything you'd expect. Only the young miss wasn't in the least bit bored. Most of the time, I rowed her very late at night. There was something even poetic about it. All night long, the western sky would be greenish, transparent, and there, on the horizon—just like now—everything somehow glimmered and glimmered . . . I could find only one oar, which looked like a shovel, and would paddle with it as if I were a savage of some kind—first on the right, then on the left. Small woods darkened the opposite shore. Beyond them, this strange twilight would continue to shine throughout the night. And an unimaginable stillness would be everywhere—only the mosquitoes whined and dragonflies flew by. I had never known that they flew late at night. I later found out that they did so for a reason. It was really frightening.''

At last, the two could hear the sound of the approaching train. It swept along with a windy roar, blended into one golden strip on the shining windows, and passed by. The coach immediately lurched as it began to move. The attendant entered the compartment, turned on the light, and started making the beds.

"Well, go on. What happened between you and that young miss? Was it a real romance? For some reason, you've never told me about her. What was she like?''

"Thin, tall. She always wore a yellow cotton sarafan. On her feet—peasant shoes woven from wool of many colors."

"And that was also in the Russian style?"

"I think it was more in the style of poverty. She didn't have anything else to wear but the sarafan. Besides, she was an artist, studying at Stroganov's School of Painting. She herself was quite picturesque, so much so that she would have made a good model for an icon. A long black braid down her back, a swarthy face with dark little moles, a thin nose, black eyes, black eyebrows . . . Her hair was dry and stiff, slightly curled. All of this against the yellow sarafan and white muslin sleeves made her look quite beautiful. Her ankles and tops of her feet weren't fleshy—the bones protruded from under the thin, dark skin."

"I know the type. I had a girl friend like that when I was taking courses. She probably got hysterical easily."

"Maybe. After all, she did have her mother's face. And her mother—some kind of princess whose family had Oriental blood—suffered from something like deep depression . . . You'd only see her at meals. She'd walk in, have a seat, say nothing, occasionally cough, never raise her eyes, continually shift her knife, then her fork. If she suddenly said something, it was always so loud and unexpected that you jumped."

"And her father?"

"He was also quiet, cold, tall—a retired soldier. Only their boy was nice, easy to get along with. He's the one I tutored."

Announcing that the beds were made, the attendant left the compartment and wished them good night.

"But what was her name?"

"Rusya."

"What kind of name is that?"

"Quite simple. It's short for Marusya."

"Well, what about it then? Were you in love, really in love with her?"

"Of course. At the time, I thought I was madly in love with her."

"And what about her?"

He grew silent, then answered drily:

"She probably felt the same. But let's go to bed. I'm exhausted after today."

"Real nice! So I got interested for nothing. Well, tell me in at least two words how your romance ended."

"There wasn't really anything to it. I went away and that was that."

"But why didn't you marry her?"

"I apparently had a premonition that one day I'd meet you."

"No, seriously?"

"Well, then, the affair was over when I shot myself and she stabbed herself with a dagger ... "

After washing up and brushing their teeth, they shut themselves in the now-stuffy compartment and undressed. With that feeling of joy experienced by travelers, they lay beneath the fresh, glossy linen sheets, lay on those pillows which were continually slipping off the raised heads of their beds.

The little violet-blue eye above the door was looking peacefully into the darkness. She fell asleep. But he lay there, smoked, and visualized that summer ...

Rusya had many small black moles all over her body—it was a unique feature of great charm. Because she walked around in soft, flat shoes, her whole body jiggled beneath the yellow sarafan. It was broad, light-weight—her long, virginal body could move freely within it. She once got her feet soaked in the rain and ran from the garden into the living room. He rushed to take her shoes off and kiss the wet, narrow feet. He'd never been as happy in his entire life. The fresh, aromatic rain sounded ever faster, ever thicker on the balcony outside the open doors. In the darkened house, everyone was sleeping after having eaten lunch. And the two of them were terribly frightened by a rooster with a large fiery comb and black feathers flecked with a metallic green. It suddenly ran in from the garden and tapped its claws along the floor at precisely that most passionate moment when they had cast all caution aside. Seeing them jump from the divan, the rooster hurriedly bowed, as if realizing he had intruded upon a delicate situation, and ran back into the rain with his shiny tail between his legs.

In the beginning, she had constantly scrutinized him. When he would start talking to her, she'd turn a deep red and reply in sarcastic mumbles. She often insulted him at the dinner table, turning to her father and saying loudly:

"Don't offer him anything, Papa. It's no use. He doesn't like cheese dumplings. He also doesn't like cold *kvass* soup, doesn't like noodles, despises yoghurt, and hates cottage cheese."

In the mornings, he would be busy with the boy, she with the housework—she was the one who ran the house. They'd have lunch at one. After that, she'd go to her room upstairs or—if it weren't raining—into the garden, where her easel stood beneath a birch. Shooing the mosquitoes away, she'd paint nature scenes, then go to the balcony, where he'd be sitting after lunch, sitting in a slanting wicker armchair with a book in his hand. She'd stand with her arms behind her back and smile vaguely at him:

"And what bits of wisdom are you pleased to be studying?"

"This history of the French Revolution."

"Oh, God! I had no idea we had a revolutionary in the house!"

"But why have you left your painting?"

"I'm soon going to give it up entirely. I'm convinced I don't have any talent."

"Show me some of your work."

"Do you think you understand anything about painting?"

"You're awfully conceited."

"That sin exists . . . "

One day, she finally asked him to take her rowing on the lake. She suddenly said with determination:

"It looks like the rainy season's over in these tropics. Let's have some fun. I know our dugout's falling to pieces and even has holes in the bottom. But Petya and I've stuffed them with marsh grass."

The day was hot, steamy. Along the shores, the humid warmth—in a stifling sort of way—heated the grasses spotted with little yellow blossoms. Countless greenish-white moths hovered just above them. Getting used to the continual mocking tone of her voice, he said as he approached the boat:

"At last you've come down to my level!"

"At least you've gotten around to answering me!" she glibly replied and jumped on the bow of the boat, frightening the frogs which splashed from all directions into the water. But suddenly she shrieked wildly, pulling the sarafan up to her knees, stamping her feet:

"A snake! A grass snake!"

He glimpsed at the shining darkness of her naked legs, then grabbed the oar from the bow, struck the grass snake coiled on the bottom of the boat, hooked it around the oar, and tossed it far out into the water.

She was pale with a kind of Indian paleness. The moles of her face had become darker, the blackness of her hair and eyes seemed somehow blacker. She sighed in relief:

"Oh, how disgusting! No wonder the word 'horror' comes from 'grass snake'! We've got them all over the place —here, in the garden, and under the house. Can you imagine, Petya even *holds* them in his hands!"

For the first time, she was talking sincerely to him. For the first time, they looked into each other's eyes.

"You're a good guy! You really smacked him!"

Then she completely regained her composure, smiled, ran

from the bow to the stern, and gaily sat down. He'd been struck by her beauty when she was frightened. Now he thought a while, with a feeling of tenderness, and said to himself, "She's really just a little girl!" But with a look of indifference, he stepped into the boat as if thinking about something else. Leaning on the oar jammed into the spongy bottom of the lake, he turned the boat around and caused it to drag through the tangled thickness of underwater weeds over green, brush-like marsh grasses, over blooming water lilies which covered everything just ahead of the boat with their fat, round leaves. He pushed the boat out onto the water, and sat on the middle seat paddling on the right, then the left.

"Isn't it nice!" she shouted.

"I'll say!" he replied, took off his cap, and turned to face her. "Please be so kind as to throw this somewhere near you," he said, "or I'll knock it off into this trough which—if you'll pardon me—is still leaking and full of leeches."

She put the cap on her knees.

"On second thought, don't worry about it. Throw it wherever you like."

She squeezed the hat to her breast:

"No, I'll protect it!"

Once more, his heart quivered tenderly, but he again turned around and began paddling hard through the sparkling water surrounded by marsh grass and water lilies.

Mosquitoes stuck to his face and hands. The warm, silver sunlight blinded everything on all sides. The steamy air. The sun lighter, then darker. The curling whiteness of clouds shining softly in the sky, reflected in the water amid islands of marsh grass and water lilies. Everywhere, the water was so shallow that he could see weeds on the bottom. Yet it still gave the impression of bottomless depth as it reflected the sky and clouds.

She suddenly shrieked again, and the boat tipped to one side. She'd stuck her hand over the back of the boat into the water. Grabbing the stem of a water lily, she'd pulled it so hard that she'd fallen over along with the boat—he was barely able to jump up and catch her under the arms. She roared with laughter, fell on her back near the stern, and splashed him in the eyes with her wet hand. Then he grabbed he once more and—not understanding what he was doing—kissed her laughing lips. She quickly embraced him around the neck and kissed him clumsily on the cheek . . .

From that time on, they went out in the boat late every night. The following day, after lunch, she called him to the garden and asked:

"Do you love me?"

He answered passionately, remembering the previous day's kisses in the boat:

"I've loved you since I first saw you!"

"And I . . . " she said. "No, at first I hated you. You didn't seem to notice me at all. But thank God, that's all over now. Tonight, when the rest of them have gone to bed, go there again and wait for me. Only be careful when you leave the house—Mama watches every step I take. She's insanely jealous."

Late that night, she arrived at the shore carrying a rug over her arm. Joyfully confused, he met her, then asked:

"Why the rug?"

"Don't be so stupid! We're going to get cold. Well, hurry up. Sit down and row us to the other shore . . . "

They were silent as they crossed the lake. As they drifted up to the woods on the other shore, she said:

"Well, here we are. Now come to me. Where's the rug? Oh, it's under my seat. Cover me up—I'm shivering—and sit down. That's the way . . . No, wait. Yesterday we kissed like we didn't know what we were doing. Now I'll kiss first, only gently, so gently. And you embrace me, touch me— everywhere . . . "

She was wearing only a slip under the sarafan. She kissed him gently, barely touching the edge of his lips. His mind swirling, he pushed her down onto the bottom of the boat near the stern. She deliriously embraced him . . .

She lay there exhausted for a while. Then she sat up. Smiling with happy weariness, with that pain she could yet feel, she said:

"Now we are man and wife. Mama says my marriage will kill her. But I don't want to think about that now . . . You know, I want to take a bath. I just love taking baths like this late at night . . . "

She pulled her clothes off over her head. The entire length of her long body became white in the darkness. She started wrapping her braid around her head, lifting her hands, exposing the dark underarms and rising breasts. She was not ashamed of her nakedness or of the dark, narrow little patch beneath her abdomen. Having tied her hair up, she quickly kissed him, jumped up, fell into the water with a splash, tossed her head back, and kicked noisily.

Later, he hurriedly helped her get dressed, and wrapped her in the rug. It was like a fairy tale—her black eyes, the black hair of the braid visible in the darkness. He dared touch her no more, only kissed her hands and remained silent, unbearably happy. All the while, he had a feeling that someone was there in the darkness of the woods, there near the shore where fireflies were now quietly glowing. He had a feeling that someone was standing there—listening. Occasionally, something would make a cautious rustle. She looked up:

"Stop—what was that?"

"Don't worry. It's probably a frog crawling onto the shore. Or a grass snake in the woods . . . "

"But what if it's a goat?"

"What kind of goat?"

"I don't know. But just think of it—a goat of some kind comes out of the woods, stands there and watches us . . . I feel so good I just want to start blabbing the stupidest things I can think of!"

And he again pressed her hands to his lips. He kept kissing her cold breast as if it were something holy. What an entirely new being she had become! The greenish twilight—not yet extinguished—was still standing beyond the blackness of woods lying close to the earth. That light was faintly reflected in the smooth water that turned white in the distance. The vegetation along the shore had a sharp scent, like celery. The invisible mosquitoes were whining mysteriously, imploringly. Terrifying dragonflies—wide awake—were flying all around, making a quiet sound as they passed over the boat and then continued along the water, shining in the dead of night. And all the while something, somewhere was making a noise, a rustling noise. It was crawling, winding its way through the woods . . .

A week later, he was thrown out of the house in an ugly, shameful manner. He was stunned by the horror of a separation so abrupt.

Shortly after lunch, both of them were sitting in the dining room. Heads touching, they were looking at pictures in old issues of *Niva*.

"You still love me, don't you?" he asked quietly, pretending to be looking at the pictures.

"Stupid man. You're awfully stupid!" she whispered.

They suddenly heard feet running, running softly—and her deranged mother appeared in the doorway in a frayed, black silk robe and worn slippers of morocco leather. There was something tragic in her sparkling eyes. She ran in theatrically and cried out:

"I know exactly what's going on! I sensed it, I've followed you. You bum, *you* won't have her!"

She raised her arm in its long sleeve and fired a deafening shot from the antique pistol Petya used to scare sparrows away. The boy had loaded it with only gunpowder. The young man lunged in the smoke for the woman and grabbed her clenched hand. She tore herself free, gashed his forehead with the pistol, then hurled it at him. As she heard other people in the house running to the sounds of the screams and pistol shot, she started shouting even more theatrically, with foam on her blue-gray lips:

"She'll run to you over my dead body! The day she runs off with you, I'll hang myself, do you hear me, hang myself! I'll jump off the roof! Get out of my house, you bum! Marya Viktorovna, choose—your mother or him!"

"You, Mama, you . . . "

He woke up, opened his eyes—from the black darkness, the little eye of violet-blue above the door was still looking at him with that same enigmatic, funereal stare. And with the same steady motion, the coach quickly lunged, rocking on its springs.

They had already left that little halfway station far, far behind. And the story had taken place a whole twenty years earlier—the woods, magpies, marsh, water lilies, grass snakes, cranes . . . Yes, there had even been cranes—how could he have forgotten them! During that amazing summer, everything had been strange. The pair of cranes were even strange. They had occasionally flown in from somewhere and landed on the marsh's shore. It was strange how they would let only her come near them. Curving their thin, long necks, they would watch her with a look of austere, yet affectionate curiosity as she gently ran up to them in her multicolored peasant shoes, squatted in front of them— spreading the hem of her yellow sarafan down over the damp, warm vegetation near the shore—and with childlike enthusiasm looked into the beautiful, threatening pupils of their little eyes, lined by thin rings of dark-gray.

From a distance, he had watched her and the cranes through binoculars. And he had distinctly seen the birds' small, shining heads, even their bony nostrils, the slits in their large, strong beaks, which they used to kill grass snakes in a single blow. Their stubby bodies with the fluffy down on their tails were covered with a tight, steely plumage. Their scaly, cane-like legs were disproportionately long and thin. The legs of one were totally black, while those of the other were greenish. Sometimes, one or the other would jump around for no apparent reason, spreading its immense wings. And they'd strut with an air of importance, walk with slow, measured steps, lift their claws while pressing three of their toes into a ball. Then they'd stretch those toes just like birds of prey do, all the while nodding their little heads . . .

But whenever she ran up to them, he no longer thought about anything, but only saw her sarafan spread over the ground. He trembled in a death-like stupor at the thought of her dark body underneath the sarafan, of the little dark moles. And on that last day when they had been together, the last time they sat next to each other on the living room divan while looking at an old issue of *Niva,* she had again held his cap in her hands and clutched it to her breast, just as she had once done in the boat. And as she looked into his eyes with her eyes—like a dark mirror, sparkling with joy— she said:

"I love you so much that even the smell inside your cap, the smell of your head, the smell of your awful cologne means more to me than anything in the whole wide world!"

They were eating lunch in the dining car somewhere on the other side of Kursk. After he'd finished drinking coffee with brandy, his wife said to him:

"Why are you drinking so much? That's your fifth glass, isn't it? Are you still sad about your dacha girl with the bony feet?"

"I am, I am," he replied laughing unpleasantly. "My dacha girl . . . *Amata nobis quantum amabitur nulla!*"

"Is that Latin? What's it mean?"

"You don't need to know."

"You've got such bad manners," she said, sighed a careless sigh, and began looking out the sunny window.

[1940]

The Beauty

A CIVIL SERVANT IN THE province's Department of Revenue. A widower. Middle-aged. Married a young woman, a beauty, the daughter of a military commander. He was reserved, timid, and she knew that she was quite something. He was thin, tall, prone to tuberculosis, wore iodine-colored glasses, talked somewhat hoarsely and—if he wanted to speak louder—broke into a falsetto. And she wasn't large. Built firmly, superbly. Always well-dressed. Very attentive and confident around the house. Kept an eagle eye on everything. Like many provincial bureaucrats, he seemed to have little interest in any personal relationships. Even his first marriage had been to a beauty. And all just threw up their hands and asked, "What do they see in him?"

And this second beauty quietly got to hate his seven-year-old boy by the first wife. She pretended she didn't notice him at all. And then the father himself, fearing her, also acted as if he never had a son. And the boy, who was by nature lively and affectionate, became afraid of saying anything when they were around. He stayed completely out of the way, as if he didn't exist.

Right after the wedding, they no longer let him sleep in

his father's bed, but moved him to a little divan in the living room, a small area near the dining room appointed with blue velvet furniture.

Yet his dreams were restless. Every night, he would kick the blanket and sheet onto the floor. And soon The Beauty told the maid:

"It's disgraceful. He's wearing off all the velvet on the divan. Nastya, make his bed on the floor, on that straw mattress I had you hide in the deceased lady's large trunk out in the hallway."

And the boy, all alone in the world, began living a totally independent life isolated from the rest of the household. Day in and day out, his life was inaudible, inconspicuous, unchanged. He would sit meekly in a corner of the living room drawing little houses on a chalkboard or whispering the syllables of the words which were in the small picture book his mother had bought him when she was still alive. And he looked out the window . . .

He slept on the floor between the divan and a potted palm. He made his own bed at night and conscientiously put it away the next morning, rolling it up and taking it to Mama's trunk in the hallway. He hid all his other things in there.

[1940]

Antigone

IN JUNE, THE STUDENT left his mother's estate to visit his uncle and aunt. He was supposed to visit them, find out how they were getting along, and how his uncle's health was. His uncle, a retired general, had lost both legs. The student fulfilled this duty every summer, and was now going there with a feeling of obedient calm. Sitting in the second-class coach, he was leisurely reading a new book by Averchenko, slinging his muscular, young thigh over the arm of the seat. He looked absentmindedly out the window at the telegraph poles rising and falling, poles with little porcelain cups resembling lilies of the valley. He appeared to be a young officer—only his white cap with its blue hatband indicated he was a student. Everything else was military—the white tunic, greenish riding breeches, boots with patent leather tops, and cigarette case bearing the insignia of a flaming orange torch.

His uncle and aunt were wealthy. Whenever he'd return home from Moscow, a cumbersome wagon would always meet him at the station. It was pulled by a team of workhorses and driven not by a coachman, but by a field hand. Yet at his uncle's station, he always entered—however briefly—a totally different world, one characterized by the joys of prosperity. He began to feel handsome, cheerful—phony. That's the way it was right now. With an unintended phoniness, he took a seat in the light-weight carriage which had rubber wheels and was harnessed to three frisky, dark-bay horses. The driver was a young coachman wearing a tight blue sleeveless coat and yellow silk shirt.

A quarter of an hour later, the troika—gentle jangling its bells and making a squishing sound as it rode along the sand around a flower bed—flew into the circular courtyard of the vast estate and pulled up in front of the porch of a spacious two-story house. The porch itself was as large as a railway platform. A tall, brawny servant came out to take the luggage. He was dressed in a black-striped red vest and half-boots. With great dexterity, the student made an unbelievable leap from the carriage. His aunt—smiling and swaying as she walked—appeared in the doorway of the vestibule. She was wearing a broad, loose dress of tussore over her large, flabby body. She had a big, sagging face, a nose like an anchor, and yellow bags under her brown eyes. She kissed him on both cheeks the way relatives do. Pretending to be glad, he pressed himself to her soft, dark hand, his mind racing all the while with the thought, "I'm going to have to lie like this for three whole days! I won't know what to do when I've got any time to myself!"

Hastily giving stock answers to his aunt's inquiries of feigned concern about his mother, he followed her into the large vestibule and glanced with a cheerful hatred at the slightly hunched body of a stuffed brown bear. With shiny little glass eyes, it stood pigeon-toed on its hind legs at the foot of the broad staircase. It obligingly held a bronze dish for calling cards in front paws studded with claws. And then the student actually came to a sudden halt as he felt a rush of joyful surprise—the plump, blue-eyed general was steadily approaching in a wheelchair. But he was being pushed by a tall, majestic beauty.

She was wearing a gray gingham dress, white pinafore,

and white scarf. Her eyes were large, gray. She sparkled all over with youth, strength, neatness, with the splendor of sleek hands and a cream-colored face. Kissing his uncle's hand, he managed to get a glimpse at the extraordinary shapeliness of her dress, of her slender legs. The general joked:

"And this is my Antigone, my benevolent guide, although I'm not blind like Oedipus, especially when it comes to attractive women. Get acquainted, young people."

She smiled faintly and answered the student's bow with only a bow of her own.

The brawny servant in the half-boots and red vest led him past the bear up the staircase of shiny dark-yellow wood that had a strip of carpet running up the middle. The servant took him down the same hallway leading to a large bedroom adjoining a marble bathroom. This time, the student was in a different room—the window of this one looked out onto the park, not the courtyard. But he walked along without looking at anything. That merry, trivial thought was still going through his mind, the thought which had entered his head as he'd been driving into the estate—"my uncle with the most honorable principles." But by now he was thinking something else—"What a woman!"

Humming, he began to shave, wash, and change his clothes. He put on trousers with suspenders while thinking:

"Then there really *are* women like that! Just think what a person would give up for the love of such a woman! Why is beauty like that pushing old men and women around in wheelchairs?!"

And ridiculous ideas began coming to mind:

"Well, I'll up and stay here a month, two months, secretly become her friend, get close to her, get her to love me, then say, 'Marry me! I'll be yours forever—all of me!' Mama, Aunt, Uncle, their astonishment when I announce our love, our decision to unite our lives, their indignation, then their attempts to persuade me to change my mind, shouts, tears, swearing, disinheritance—all this is nothing to me if only I can have you . . . "

Running down the staircase to see his aunt and uncle—their rooms were downstairs—he thought:

"But that's really a bunch of nonsense! Of course, I could stay here under any pretext I could think up . . . I could start pretending to be madly in love . . . But what would you get out of it? And if you did get anything, where would you go from there? How would the story end? Would you actually get married?"

For about an hour, he sat with his aunt and uncle in his uncle's enormous study with its enormous desk, its enormous ottoman upholstered with fabric from Turkestan. A carpet hung on the wall above the ottoman. Crossed rifles from the Orient were on another wall. There were small inlaid tables for guests to sit at while smoking, and on the mantle was a large portrait photograph in a rosewood frame topped with a golden crown. The photograph had been personally signed with a flourish: "Alexander."

As the conversation was nearing an end, the student was thinking of the nurse when he said, "I'm so happy, Uncle and Aunt, to be with you once again. How marvelous your beautiful home is! I will be dreadfully unhappy to leave."

"But who's running you off?" his uncle answered. "Where are you rushing off to? Live it up until you get bored."

"Of course," his aunt said absentmindedly.

As he was sitting and talking, he expected her to come in at any moment. The maid would announce that tea would be served in the dining room, and She would come in to push his uncle's wheelchair. Instead, tea was served in the study. A maid rolled in a table bearing a silver teapot heated by a spirit lamp. His aunt did the pouring herself. He then started hoping she would bring his uncle some medicine, any kind of medicine. But she didn't appear.

"Well, to hell with her!" he thought as he left the study

for the dining room, where a maid was lowering the blinds of the tall, sunny windows. For some reason, she was looking to the right, through the door of the parlor, where the sun of early evening was reflected in the glass coasters pinned to the floor by the legs of the piano. Then he passed to the left, into the living room, which led to the den. He walked from the living room out onto the balcony, went down toward a bed of brightly colored flowers, walked around it, and plodded along a shady path lined with tall trees. It was still hot in the sun, and dinner would not be served for another two hours.

At seven-thirty, the gong began howling in the vestibule. He was the first to enter the dining room, sparkling festively in the light of the chandelier. Already standing near a small table by a wall were the plump, shaven cook dressed all in starched white; a sunken-cheeked footman wearing white crocheted gloves; and a petite maid who was slender in a French sort of way. A minute later, the aunt walked in, swaying, looking like a queen with her milk-white hair. She was wearing a pale-yellow silk dress trimmed with cream-colored lace. He could see masses of flesh on her ankles above her tight silk slippers. And she was underneath all of this. But as she pushed her husband up to the table, she immediately glided from the room without turning to the student. He was only able to notice something strange about her eyes—they weren't blinking.

Wearing a general's light-gray, double-breasted jacket decorated with small crosses, the uncle crossed himself. The aunt and student fervently crossed themselves while standing, then sat down and unfolded their shining napkins as if they were at someone's birthday party. The uncle was quite obviously ill as he sat there withering away, pale, with his damp, watery hair neatly combed. Yet he talked with style and ate a lot as he discussed the war—this was the time of the Russo-Japanese War. ("Why the hell did we start it?")

The footman performed his duties with an attitude of

offended apathy. The maid assisted him as she took short steps with her exquisite little legs. With the look of importance one sees on the face of a statue, the cook lowered the dishes. They ate a piping-hot fish soup, bloody roast beef, young potatoes sprinkled with dill. They drank the red and white wine which Prince Golitsyn, one of the uncle's old friends, had given them. The student talked, replied, smiled gaily while he agreed—just like a parrot—with all the ridiculous ideas he had recently adopted and been pretending were his own. And he was thinking, "But where is She having dinner? Is she really eating with the maid?" And he counted the minutes as he waited for her to return to take his uncle away, and later meet him somewhere. He thought how the two of them would exchange only a few words. But she came in, turned the wheelchair from the table, pushed it toward the door, and once again disappeared.

Late that night, the nightingales sang cautiously, zealously in the park. The freshness of the air, the dew, the watered flowers in the flower beds came in through the open windows. The bed sheets of Dutch linen turned cold.

The student was lying in the darkness. He'd already decided to face the wall and fall asleep, but suddenly raised his head and sat up. He threw off the covers and saw a small door at the head of his bed. Curious, he turned its key and found another door behind it. He tried this one too, but it seemed to be locked from the other side. Someone was right then walking softly behind those doors, doing something in a secretive way. He held his breath, slid from the bed, opened the first door, and listened carefully. Something began making a quiet sound on the floor behind the door . . .

He grew cold. "Could this really be her room?" He pressed his face to the keyhole. Fortunately, the key was not in it. He saw light, the edge of a woman's dresser, then something white suddenly standing up and blocking the entire view . . . No doubt about it—it was her room. Whose else could it be? They wouldn't put the maid in there. And Marya Ilinishna, his aunt's old maid, slept downstairs near the mistress's bedroom. And he almost became instantly ill from the late-night nearness of the woman who was right behind this wall, ill because he couldn't get to her. He didn't sleep for a long time. A little later, he woke up and still had the same feeling, visualized her, pictured her sheer nightgown, bare feet in their slippers . . .

"I've got to get away from here now!" he thought, and lit a cigarette.

They all drank coffee in their rooms the next morning. He had his coffee while sitting in his uncle's baggy nightshirt and silk robe. Throwing open his robe, he sadly scrutinized his body with a feeling of futility.

Lunch in the dining room was depressing and dull. He and his aunt were the only ones at the table. The weather was bad. Outside the windows, the trees swayed in the wind. Above them, cirrus clouds and storm clouds were piling up.

"Well, my dear, I'm going to have to leave you," his aunt said, standing up and crossing herself. "Entertain yourself anyway you can. You'll have to excuse your uncle and me for our frailties. We sit by ourselves until tea. It's probably going to rain, but you could still go horseback riding."

He cheerfully replied:

"Don't worry, Aunt, I'll do some reading . . . "

And he strode toward the den, where the walls were lined with book shelves.

Passing though the living room, he thought that maybe he should still have a horse saddled. But through the windows he could see storm clouds of various shapes. He could see an unpleasant azure among the violet clouds in the thrashing treetops. The cozy den smelled of cigar smoke. Beneath the book shelves, leather divans lined three walls. He read the spines of several marvelously bound books and sat down helplessly, sinking into a divan. Yes, he was bored as hell. If he could just see her, have a few words with her . . . If he could just find out what her voice was like, what kind of person she was, if she was stupid or very clever—modestly playing a role until she had her chance. More than likely, the bitch carefully watched every step she took. She was probably conceited, probably stupid more than anything else . . . But was she something! And he would have to spend another night next door to her!

He got up, opened the glass door out onto the stone steps leading to the park, heard the warbling of nightingales above the park's rustle, but was then so suddenly struck by the cool wind rushing in from the young trees off to his left that he jumped back into the room. The den grew dark, the wind whipped the trees, bending their branches of fresh green. The glass door and the windows began sparkling with sharp-pointed spatters of light rain.

"They don't mind it!" he said loudly, listening to the distant, then nearby, warbling of nightingales being lofted on that wind swirling in from all directions. Just then he heard a steady voice:

"Good afternoon."

He glanced around, panic-stricken—She was standing in the room.

"I came to exchange this book for another," she said in a cordial, impassive manner. "Books are my only joy," she added with a faint smile, turning to a book shelf.

He mumbled:

"Good afternoon. I didn't hear you come in . . ."

"Very soft carpets," she answered. And as she turned around, she was already gazing at him with her gray, unblinking eyes.

"What do you like to read?" he asked, responding with a little more courage.

"Right now, I'm reading Maupassant, Octave Mirbeau . . ."

"Yes, I can understand that. All women like Maupassant. He always writes about love."

"But what could be better than love?"

Her voice was modest, her eyes smiling softly.

"Love, love!" he said with a sigh. "There are encounters you wouldn't believe, but... What is your name and patronymic, nurse?"

"Katerina Nikolayevna. And yours?"

"Just call me Pavlik," he replied, growing bolder all the time.

"Do you think I'd make a good aunt for you?"

"What I wouldn't give for such an aunt! So far, I'm only your unhappy neighbor."

"Is it all that unhappy?"

"I heard you late last night. It turns out your room is right next to mine."

She smiled indifferently:

"And I heard you. It's not nice to eavesdrop and peep through keyholes."

"There should be a law against beauty such as yours!" he said, staring into the gray flecks of her eyes, at her cream-white face, the luster of her dark hair beneath the white scarf.

"Do you think so? And you want to stop me from being this way?"

"I do. Your hands alone could drive a man crazy... "

And with light-hearted boldness, he grabbed her right hand with his left. Standing with her back against the book shelves, she glanced over his shoulder into the living room. She didn't take her hand away, but looked at him with a strange smile—as if waiting—a smile that asked, "Well, what now?" He didn't let go of her hand, but squeezed it tightly, pushed it downwards, and seized her waist in his right arm. She again glanced over his shoulder, and tilted her head away slightly, as if protecting if from a kiss. Yet she pressed her arching waist against his body. Breathing

127

hoarsely, he stretched for her half-closed lips and pressed her toward the divan. Frowning, she shook her head and whispered, "No, no. We can't lying down. We couldn't see if anyone was coming. We couldn't hear anything . . . " And with eyes that had lost their sparkle, she slowly moved her legs apart . . .

A minute later, his face sagged onto her shoulder. She was still standing, clenching her teeth. She gently freed herself from him, then walked steadily through the living room, saying in a loud, indifferent voice above the sound of the rain:

"Oh, what rain! And all the windows upstairs are open . . . "

The next morning, he woke up in her bed. Wearing a slip, she had rolled away from him early in the morning, lain on the sheet bunched up under her back, and rested a bare arm under her head. He opened his eyes and joyfully met her unblinking gaze. So dizzy he almost fainted, he sensed the sharp scent of her underarm . . .

Someone hurriedly knocked at the door.

"Who's there?" she asked calmly, not pushing him away. "Is that you, Marya Ilinishna?"

"It's me, Katerina Nikolayevna."

"What is it?"

"Please let me in. I'm afraid someone will hear me, run off and tell the General's wife . . . "

As he jumped into his room, she slowly turned the key in the lock.

"His Excellency's not so good. I think he needs an injection," Marya Ilinishna whispered as she came in. "Thank God the General's wife is still asleep. Go right away . . . "

Marya Ilinishna's eyes were already as round as a snake's. While she was talking, she suddenly spotted a man's slippers near the bed—the student had run out in his bare feet. And the nurse also spotted the slippers—and Marya Ilinishna's eyes.

Before lunch, the nurse went to the General's wife and told her that she had to leave right away. She began to lie serenely, saying that she had received a letter from her father, news that her brother had been seriously wounded in Manchuria and that her widowed father was all alone in his grief . . .

"Oh, how I do understand!" the General's wife said, having already learned everything from Marya Ilinishna. "Well, what's to be done? Go. Only telegraph Dr. Krivtsov from the station. Ask him to come right away and stay here until we can find another nurse . . . "

Then the nurse knocked on the student's door and shoved a note under it. The note read:

> They found out. I'm going away. The old woman saw your slippers by the bed. Don't think ill of me.

At lunch, the aunt was only a little sad, yet talked to him as if nothing had happened.

"Did you hear? The nurse is going away to stay with her father. Her brother was frightfully wounded, and the father is alone . . . "

"I heard all about it, Aunt. What unhappiness this war is, how much sorrow everywhere. But what was the matter with Uncle?"

"Oh, thank God, it's nothing serious. He's just a terrible hypochondriac. It's like it's his heart, but it's all caused by his stomach . . . "

At three o'clock, a troika carried Antigone to the station. Not looking up, he said goodbye to her on the long porch as if he'd accidentally bumped into her while running to have a horse saddled. He was ready to start weeping in despair. She waved a glove to him from the carriage, sitting there no longer wearing a scarf, but a nice hat.

[1940]

A Little Fool

THE DEACON'S SON, A SEM-
inarian, came home to see his parents over the holidays.
One dark, hot night, he was awakened by a sharp stirring in
his body. As he lay there for a long time, his imagination
was inflamed with a fantasy even more intense: He pictured
himself in the afternoon, before dinner, peeking from
behind a thicket of willows growing near the banks of a
creek. Girls who had walked there from work were taking
their blouses off their sweaty white bodies. Pulling them
over their heads, they were tossing them aside. He watched
them making all kinds of noise, laughing loudly, scratching
their faces, arching their backs, and rushing into the hot,
sparkling water . . .

No longer able to control himself, he got up from his bed
and stole in the darkness through the front hallway into the
kitchen. Black and hot in there, it felt like the inside of a
warm oven. He began fumbling around, reaching for the
bunk where the cook was sleeping. She was a destitute,
homely girl known for being a little fool. Because he frightened her so, she didn't even cry out. After that, he lived with
her for the rest of the summer.

She bore him a son, who began his life in the kitchen near

his mother. The deacon, the deaconess, the priest, and the whole household knew who the boy's father was. And the seminarian, coming home for the holidays, couldn't even look at him without feeling wicked shame for what he had done. He had lived with the little fool!

After he had graduated—"Brilliantly!" the deacon told everyone—he again came to see his parents. It was the summer before he was to begin study at the academy. On the very first holiday, the deacon and deaconess invited guests to tea to show off their future academician. The guests also spoke of his brilliant future, drank tea, and ate all sorts of jams. In the midst of this animated conversation, the happy deacon wound up a gramophone which sputtered, then cried out. Everyone grew silent and with smiles of satisfaction listened to the strains of "Along a Paved Street," which seemed to wash away all cares.

Suddenly, the cook's son flew into the room, clumsily stamping his feet, dancing out of rhythm. Having thought everyone would feel sorry for the boy if they saw him, the mother had stupidly whispered, "Run, child, dance!" They were all struck dumb by his unexpected appearance. The deacon's son, turning scarlet, fell upon him like a tiger and hurled him from the room with such force that the boy rolled like a top into the front hallway.

The next day, the deacon and deaconess—at the seminarian's request—fired the cook. Both of them were good, compassionate people. They had grown very attached to her, were fond of her mild temperament and obedient manner. They had implored him to forgive what the cook's son had done. But he was adamant—and they dared not disobey him. By evening, the cook had gone from the front yard. As she left, she wept quietly, holding a satchel in one hand, her boy's little hand in the other.

Throughout the summer, the two of them walked through towns and villages begging alms. She wore ragged clothes, was scorched by the sun and wind, was thin as skin and bones. Yet she kept going. She walked barefooted, with a sackcloth bag slung over one shoulder. Propped up by a tall staff, she bowed silently before every *izba* in the towns and villages along the way. Walking behind her, the boy also carried a bag over one shoulder. The old shoes he wore were falling apart. They had become hard, the kind of discarded shoes that used to lie around in the ravine.

He was ugly. The top of his head was large and flat, in a shock of red wool. He had a pug nose with broad nostrils, eyes like walnuts that shone with great brilliance. Yet when he smiled, he was quite handsome.

[1940]

Galya Ganskaya

THE ARTIST AND THE former sailor were sitting together on the terrace of a Paris café. It was April, and the artist was enjoying the weather. How beautiful Paris was in the springtime, how charming the Parisian ladies were in those first, elegant dresses of spring!

"In my own Golden Age, Paris was of course even more beautiful in the spring," he said. "It wasn't just because I was young. Paris then was something altogether different. Just think—not a single automobile. But life in the city went on then just as it does now!"

"Yet for some reason, I recall springtime in Odessa," the sailor said. "You're from Odessa. You can remember better than I its unique charm—that blend of a sun already hot and the still-wintry freshness of the sea, the bright sky, and spring clouds above the sea. And on days like this, the ladies' spring fashions on the Deribasovskaya . . . "

Lighting his pipe, the artist shouted, "*Garçon, un demi!*" and turned excitedly to the sailor:

"Pardon me. I interrupted you. Just imagine—while I'm talking about Paris, I'm also thinking about Odessa. You're absolutely right. Spring in Odessa really is something unique. But I always remember the springtimes in Paris and Odessa somehow mixed together. They alternate in my mind. After all, you remember that back then I often went to Paris in the spring . . . Remember Galya Ganskaya? You'd seen her somewhere and told me you'd never met a more charming girl. Don't you remember? Well, it doesn't matter. As I was talking of that Paris of long ago, I just remembered her and that spring in Odessa when she first dropped by my studio. Each one of us probably remembers a love we have particularly cherished or a particularly oppressive amorous sin. And so it seems that Galya is my most beautiful recollection and my most oppressive sin, even though God knows I didn't commit it on purpose. The affair took place so long ago that now I can be totally frank in telling you about it . . .

"I knew her when I was still a teenager. She grew up without a mother, with her father, whom her mother had long since abandoned. He was well-to-do, an unsuccessful artist by profession. He was an amateur, as they say, but such a passionate one—nothing in the world interested him but painting. Throughout his life, he'd devoted himself only to whatever stood on the other side of his easel. He crammed his house—he had an estate in Otrada—with both old and new paintings. He bought up everything he liked, from all over, wherever possible. He was very handsome— plump, tall, with a marvelous bronzed beard. Half-Polish, half-Ukrainian. He lived like a great lord, proud, polite in a refined sort of way. The man was really quite reserved, yet gave the impression of being very extroverted, especially with us. All of us young Odessa artists used to visit him. We went in a group to his place every Sunday for two years on end. And he always greeted us with outstretched arms. Despite the age difference, he always acted as if we were equals, talked incessantly about painting, and treated us royally.

"Galya was about thirteen or fourteen at the time, and delighted us, of course, only as a little girl does. She was sweet, playful, occasionally graceful, a small face with light-brown curls along her cheeks, just like the face of an angel. But she was such a flirt! Once, she rushed to her father as he was sitting in his studio, whispered something in his ear, then immediately jumped back. And he told us:

" 'Oh, my, dear friends, you don't know the kind of little girl that is growing up here. I fear for her!'

"Later, with the bad manners of youth, every single one of us suddenly decided to stop visiting him. We'd somehow grown tired of Otrada. It was probably because of his unending conversations about art and his latest discovery of yet another remarkable secret of painting technique. It was then I left without delay for Paris, where I spent two spring-times. As far as love affairs were concerned, I imagined I was a second Maupassant. Returning to Odessa, I would walk around like the worst possibly phony—a top hat, pea-green overcoat reaching to my knees, cream-colored gloves, boots which were half patent leather and had small buttons, an astonishing walking stick. Add to this a wavy moustache—also like Maupassant's—and a way of treating women that was despicably irresponsible.

"And so one marvelous April day, I was walking down the Deribasovskaya, crossed the Preobrazhenskaya, and at the corner near Libman's Coffee Shop suddenly ran into Galya. You remember the five-story building at the corner where that coffee shop was—at the corner of Preobrazhen-skaya and Cathedral Square. Everyone knew it because on sunny spring days chirping starlings would for some reason line its eaves. This was extraordinarily pleasant and gay.

"And now imagine if you will: Spring. Many well-dressed, carefree, friendly people all around. Those sparrows strewing their ceaseless chirping as if it were some kind of sunny rain. And Galya. And I was no longer a teenager—no longer an angel. And an astonishingly attractive, slender young woman wearing brand-new, light-gray

135

spring clothing. Beneath the small gray hat, the little face half-covered with an ashen veil—aquamarine eyes shining through. Well, of course, there were exclamations, questions, reproaches:

" 'How you all forgot Papa! How long it's been since you came to see us!'

" 'Oh, yes,' I said, 'it's been so long that you've managed to grow up.'

"Right then, I bought her a bouquet of violets from a ragged little girl. Her eyes quickly smiled in appreciation, and she instantly pressed the flowers to her face, as all women do.

" 'Would you like to sit down? Would you care for some hot chocolate?'

" 'With pleasure.'

"She raised her veil, drank the chocolate, glanced at me playfully from time to time, and asked all about Paris. All the while, I was looking at her.

" 'Papa works from morning till night. Do you work a lot, or have you fallen in love with all the Parisian ladies?'

" 'No, I don't fall in love with them anymore. I'm working now and have painted several respectable little things. Do you want to see my studio? It would be all right—after all, you're the daughter of an artist, and I live only two steps from here.'

"She was overjoyed:

" 'Of course it would be all right! Besides, I've never been in a studio except Papa's!'

"She lowered the veil and grabbed her parasol. We walked arm in arm, she stepped on my foot along the way and laughed.

" 'Galya,' I said, 'after all, may I call you Galya?'

"She immediately replied in a serious tone:

" 'You may.'

" 'Galya, what's to be done with you?'

" 'What do you mean?'

" 'You always were charming, but now you're so charming it's simply astonishing!'

"She again stepped on my foot and said not in a joking manner, yet not seriously, 'There's even more to come!'

"Do you remember the dark, narrow staircase that led from the courtyard to my tower? She suddenly grew silent here, her silk slip rustling as she walked, and all the time looking around at everything. She entered the studio almost reverently, and whispered, 'O-o-h, how nice you've got it here! Hidden away. And what a monstrous divan! And you've done so many paintings, and all of Paris . . . ' She moved with silent delight from painting to painting, forcing herself to linger, to examine each one. Having seen as much as she wanted to, she said with a sigh:

" 'Yes, you've done so many beautiful things!'

" 'Would you care for a small glass of port and some cookies?'

" 'I don't know . . . '

"I took her parasol, tossed it onto the divan, and held her little hand in its white kid glove.

" 'May I kiss it?'

" 'But I still have my glove on . . . '

"I unbuttoned the glove and kissed the base of her small palm. She lowered her veil, peered through it with expressionless aquamarine eyes, and said softly:

" 'Well, it's time for me to go.'

" 'No,' I said, 'let's first sit down for a little while. I still haven't had a chance to get a good look at you.'

"I sat down and had her sit on my lap. Can you imagine that this ravishing female wasn't the least bit heavy? She asked me somewhat enigmatically:

" 'Do you like me?'

"I looked her over, noticing the violets she'd pinned to her new little jacket, and was so touched by the sight that I broke out laughing.

" 'Do you like these violets?' I asked.

" 'I don't understand.'

" 'What don't you understand? You're just like these violets.'

"Lowering her eyes, she laughed:

" 'In our Gymnasium, we said that people who compared ladies to different flowers were scribblers.'

" 'That might be, but how else would you describe it?'

" 'I don't know . . . '

"And she gently dangled her fashionable little legs and sparkled her small, half-opened, childlike lips . . . I lifted the veil, tilted her head back, and kissed her—she tilted it back a little more. I moved my hand up the slippery, greenish silk stocking, but it was fastened at its elastic top. I undid it, and kissed the warm pink body where her thigh began, then again kissed her little half-opened mouth. She began to nibble my lips so slightly . . . "

The sailor shook his head and smiled:

"*Vieux satyr!*"

"Don't say such foolish things!" the artist said. "It's very painful for me to recall all this!"

"Well, all right, keep going."

"After that, I didn't see her for a whole year. And then one day—also in the spring—I finally got around to walking to Otrada, where Gansky greeted me with such touching joy that I burned with shame remembering how swinishly we had forsaken him. He'd aged a great deal—there was silver in his beard—but he spoke with the same excitement about painting. He began by proudly showing me his new works —enormous golden swans flying over pale-blue sand dunes of some kind. The poor man was always trying to keep up with the times. I recklessly lied:

" 'Marvelous, marvelous! You've made great progress! It's subdued, yet beams like a boy.'

" 'Well, I'm glad, very glad indeed you like it. Now let's have some lunch!'

" 'But where's your little girl?'

" 'She went to town. You wouldn't recognize her now. She's not a little girl anymore, but is already a young woman. She's now pretty much everything but a little girl—grown up, tall, a little sprig now become a big poplar.'

"Well, I was out of luck, I thought. I'd visited the old man only because I wanted more than anything to see her. And now, as if on purpose, she was in town. I had lunch, kissed the soft, aromatic beard, promised to come the following Sunday, and left. And then I saw her, walking straight toward me. She stopped joyfully and said:

" 'It's you! What luck! Were you with Papa? I'm so glad!'

"And I told her that Papa had said it would be even more difficult for me to recognize her now, that she was no longer a little poplar, but a big one. And it was true. That was the way she really was—it was as if she were not quite yet a woman, but still a very young lady. She would smile and twirl the open parasol on her shoulder. The parasol was white, lace. The dress and large hat were also white, lace. And her hair coming out from under that hat had the most charming chestnut tint. I could no longer see that former naiveté in her eyes. Her little face was now longer . . .

" 'Yes, I'm even a little taller than you.'

"I only nodded and said, 'True, true . . . ' I then said, 'Let's go down to the sea. Let's go!' We walked down a lane between gardens. As I spoke to her, I saw that she was still feeling the shock of our unexpected meeting. I kept looking at her. She walked perfectly straight, closed her parasol, and held the lace dress in her left hand. We strolled out onto a cliff—a fresh wind was blowing. The gardens were already green, and seemed to be fainting in the sun. The sea—low waves, icy, like in the north—rolled up into a crooked green wave frosted with whitecaps. I'll spare you the details, but I can still recall the Yevksinsky Bridge sinking in the distance into the bluish haze.

"We stood there, gazing in silence, as if waiting for something. She seemed to be thinking the same thing I was thinking—how she had sat on my lap the previous year. And I clasped her around the waist, pressing her so tightly to me that she bent back. I searched for her lips, she tried to get free, twisted her head away, leaned away, and then suddenly gave her lips to me. All of this happened in silence—neither she nor I made a sound. Then she wrenched herself free, straightened her hat, and said with simplicity, with conviction:

" 'You're a real bum, a real bum.'

"She turned away and—not looking back—hurried along the path."

"Well, had anything happened in the studio or not?" the sailor asked.

"Not all the way. We had kissed each other with uncontrollable passion, and gone further after that. But then I started feeling sorry for her. Her face had become as red as an ember. Her hair was tousled. And I could see that she no longer had the same childlike control over herself—and she desperately, urgently wanted this terrible thing back. I pretended to be offended:

" 'Well, we don't have to, we don't have to, if you don't want to, we don't have to . . . '

"And I began gently kissing her little hands, and she grew calm . . . "

"But then why after all that didn't you see her again for a whole year?"

"God only knows. I was afraid that the second time I wouldn't feel sorry for her."

"Then you weren't a very good Maupassant."

"Perhaps. But wait, let me finish the story. I didn't see her again for another six months. The summer had ended, everyone had begun returning home from their dachas, even though this was the best time to be living in them—this Bessarabian autumn was somehow heavenly in the tranquillity of its hot, monotonous days, the clearness of its air, the beautiful dark blue of the calm sea, and the dry yellowness of its corn fields. Even I returned from my dacha and walked once more past Libman's. And if you can imagine it, she was again walking toward me. She approached as if nothing had happened, started laughing loudly, making a wry, yet charming, face:

" 'Here's that fatal spot again—Libman's!'

" 'Why are you so cheerful? I'm awfully glad to see you, but why are you so happy?'

" 'I don't know. After I've been to the beach, I don't always feel my legs underneath me. It's from having so much fun running all over town. I've gotten suntanned and grown a little taller, haven't I?'

"I looked at her. She was right. But more than anything else, she was as gay, as free as her conversation, her laughter. She acted as if she'd just been married. Then she suddenly asked:

" 'Do you still have port and cookies?'

" 'I do.'

" 'I'd like to see your studio again. May I?'

" 'Merciful God! You sure can!'

" 'Well, let's go then. And quickly, quickly!'

"I grabbed her on the staircase. She again leaned away, again shook her head, but wasn't resisting very much. I led her to the studio, kissing her upturned face. In the studio, she began whispering in a mysterious way:

" 'But listen, this is crazy . . . I've gone crazy . . . '

"She'd already pulled off her little straw hat and thrown it onto the seat of an armchair. Her reddish hair was piled on top of her head, pinned with a tortoiseshell comb. Bangs curled on her forehead. Her face lightly, evenly suntanned. Her eyes held a joyful, yet vacant, expression . . .

"I started to undress her, taking off anything I could. She hurriedly began helping me. In a minute, I had taken off her small, white silk blouse. As you can imagine, my eyes grew dark when I saw her pale pink body with its suntanned, shiny shoulders. The milky whiteness of the breasts uplifted by her corset. The scarlet nipples jutting out. How one after the other, she deftly pulled her slender little legs with their golden slippers from the petticoats which had fallen to the floor. The legs in delicate, cream-colored stockings, the legs in—you remember—those wide, cambric panties with a slit up the side, the kind they used to wear back then. Like an animal, I grabbed at that slit and threw her onto the pillows of the divan. Her eyes turned black, got even bigger, her lips parted deliriously . . .

"I can see it all now. She was unbelievably passionate . . . But let's leave it there. Here's what happened some two weeks later. By then, she'd been coming to my place almost every day. One morning, she unexpectedly ran into the studio and bluntly asked me from the doorway:

" 'Is it true what they're saying, that you're going away to Italy in a day or two?'

" 'Yes. So what?'

" 'Why didn't you say anything to me about it? Were you trying to sneak off?'

" 'Don't get so upset. I was just about to go to your place to tell you.'

" 'In front of Papa? Why not just tell me? No, you're *not* going anywhere!'

"I foolishly retorted:

" 'No, I *am* going.'

" 'No, you're *not!*'

" 'And I'm telling you I *am!*'

" 'And that's final?'

" 'Final. But you understand, don't you, that I'll be back in about a month, a month and a half at the most? Listen, Galya, all in all . . . '

" 'Don't call me Galya anymore—I'm Galina to you! Now I understand you. I understand everything, everything! If you started promising me right now that you would never go anywhere, I wouldn't even care. That's no longer what's really important!'

"And she threw the door open, slammed it shut with all her might. The little heels of her shoes pounded quickly on the steps as she went running down the stairs. I wanted to rush after her, but held back. 'No,' I thought, 'give her some time to come to her senses. In the evening, I'll head for Otrada, tell her I don't want to cause her any pain, that I won't go to Italy, and we'll make up.' But at about five, the artist Sinani suddenly showed up at my studio and told me with a wild look in his eyes:

" 'Do you know Gansky's little girl has poisoned herself? She's dead! God only knows what poison she swiped from him—it was something exotic, instantaneous. Remember when that old idiot showed us a whole little cupboard full of poisons? He thought he was some kind of Leonardo da Vinci! They're a crazy people, these Poles and their women! What suddenly made her do it? No one can figure it out. Her father says it's like he's been struck by a bolt from the blue . . . '

"I wanted to shoot myself," the artist said softly, grew silent, then filled his pipe with tobacco. "I almost lost my mind . . . "

[1940]

The Visitor

THE VISITOR RANG ONCE, twice. Silence behind the door. No reply. Once more, he pulled the knob, ringing the doorbell long, persistently, demandingly. The sound of heavy running footsteps. And a short wench, robust as a fish, opened the door with a look of bewilderment. She smelled all over of kitchen fumes. Lackluster hair. Cheap turquoise earrings in fat ear lobes. A Finnish face with red freckles, ripe with blue-gray blood. And, of course, greasy hands.

The visitor went on the attack quickly, angrily, and merrily:

"Why aren't you answering the door? Did you fall asleep or something?"

"Not at all. A person can't hear anything from the kitchen. The stove makes a lot of noise," she answered, continuing to look at him in dismay. He was thin, dark-complexioned, toothy, with a black, stiff goatee and penetrating eyes. Draped over his arm was a gray, silk-lined overcoat. A gray hat tilted back on his head.

"We know all about your kitchen! More than likely, a kitchen gossip is sitting back there, right?"

"Not at all."

"Well, well, well. I'll take a look for myself!"

While talking, he glanced from the front hallway into the living room, shining in the sunlight. He noticed its armchairs of rich red velvet and the portrait of a broad-cheeked Beethoven hanging between two windows.

"Well, who are you?"

"What do you mean 'who'?"

"Are you the new cook?"

"That's right . . ."

"Fekla? Fedosya?"

"Not at all . . . Sasha."

"Aren't your employers at home?"

"The master is at the editorial office, the mistress rode off to Vasilevsky Island to—what do you call it?—a Sunday School."

"How irritating. Well, nothing can be done about it. I'll come back tomorrow. Just tell them that a terrible, black gentleman came—Adam Adamych. Repeat what I just said."

"Adam Adamych."

"Right, Eve of Flanders. See that you remember. In the meantime, here's what . . ."

Again, he glanced around with an animated look and threw his overcoat on a peg near a trunk:

"Come here right this minute."

"What for?"

"You'll see . . ."

And within a minute—his hat tilted back—he'd tossed her down onto the trunk and thrown up the hem of her skirt, exposing her red woolen stockings and plump, beet-colored knees.

"Master! I'll scream so everyone can hear me!"

"Then I'll strangle you. Be quiet!"

"Master! For God's sake . . . I'm a virgin!"

"There's nothing wrong with that. Well, let's get going!"

And a minute later, he was gone. Standing by the trunk,

145

she cried gently, ecstatically. Later, she began sobbing louder and louder, sobbing long, sobbing until she got the hiccups, until lunch time, until they rang for her. The mistress arrived first. She was young, wore a pince-nez, was energetic, self-confident, quick. Walking in, she immediately asked:

"Did anyone drop by?"

"Adam Adamych."

"Did he leave a message?"

"Not at all . . . He said he'd come back tomorrow."

"Why is your face tear-stained?"

"Onions . . . "

Night in the kitchen, shining clean. New shelf paper at the edges of the shelves. The red copper of scrubbed saucepans. A little lamp burning on the table. The room still warm from the stove that had not yet cooled down. The pleasant smell of leftovers smothered in a bay leaf sauce, the smell of a nice, everyday life.

Forgetting to put out the lamp, she slept soundly behind the partition. She lay there without undressing, having fallen asleep with the sweet hope that Adam Adamych would come tomorrow, that she would see his terrible eyes, and—God willing—her employers would again not be home.

But he didn't come in the morning. And at dinner the master told the mistress:

"Do you know that Adam left for Moscow? Blagosvetlov told me. He probably dropped in yesterday to say goodbye."

[1940]

A Chapel

A HOT SUMMER DAY. IN THE field behind an old estate, a long-forgotten cemetery—knolls embroidered with tall flowers and grasses, and a solitary, dilapidated brick chapel all overgrown with wildflowers and grasses, nettles and thistles. Children from the estate, squatting at the base of the chapel, are looking closely into a long, narrow, broken window at ground level. They can't see anything in there—only cold air is blowing from within. Everywhere else it's bright and hot, but in there it's dark and cold. In there, in iron boxes, lie someone's grandfathers and grandmothers in addition to someone's uncle who shot himself. All of this is very interesting and wondrous. Out here we have the sun, flowers, grasses, flies, bumblebees, and butterflies. We can play and run. We are a little uneasy, yet we gaily squat down. But they always lie in there, in the dark—like midnight—in big, cold boxes. The grandfathers and grandmothers are all old, and the uncle is still young . . .

"But why did he shoot himself?"

"He was very much in love, and when men are very much in love they always shoot themselves . . . "

In the sky's blue sea, beautiful white clouds stand here

and there like islands. The warm wind blowing from the field carries with it the sweet smell of blossoming rye. And the hotter and more joyfully the sun beats down, the colder the air blows from the darkness, from the window.

[1944]

A Memorable Ball

THIS CHRISTMAS BALL IN Moscow was like all the others. Yet that evening, I thought everything was somehow special—the well-dressed, excited crowd, the intoxicating sounds of people rustling along the front staircase, the crush of dancers in the ballroom—its two-tiered windows reflecting the light of each chandelier crystal—and the rolling, all-consuming sound of the wood-winds triumphantly pealing in chorus.

I stood for a long time at the ballroom doors thinking only of her imminent arrival. She had told me the night before that she would come at eleven. While waiting, I was so distracted that people entering the ballroom kept bumping into me. Those leaving its already hot stuffiness had difficulty getting around me. This ballroom sultriness, as well as my anticipation of her coming—I'd at last decided to tell her something final, definite—made me feel even hotter in my clothes. My frock coat. Vest. The back of my shirt. Collar. My smoothly combed hair. Only my sweating forehead was cold, cold as ice. And I could feel its coldness, feel the bone beneath the skin, feel even the bone's whiteness, which certainly must have seemed death-like in sharp contrast with my black eyes.

My feelings intensified. My love for her had long made me ill. In a magical way, I feared her pedigreed body, her full lips, the sound of her voice, her breathing. I was afraid, I—a strong, thirty-year-old officer of the Guards who had just retired from the service! Suddenly I glanced fearfully at the clock—it was exactly eleven—and strode down the staircase toward the growing throng. A frosty cold arose from the foot of the stairs and penetrated my frock coat. It did so with an ease and subtlety which I wasn't used to—I'd worn a dress-uniform for so long.

I rushed down the staircase without looking at the crowd, ran with unusual quickness and agility. But still I was late—I found her among the new arrivals and those getting out of their coats. She'd already taken hers off, and was poised there in a black lace dress, with bared shoulders, and an Orenburg scarf thrown over her upswept hair. Her expressionless eyes were shining from beneath the scarf. Tossing it off, she silently extended her hand for me to kiss. The hand was in a white glove reaching to her elbow. I was so frightened I could hardly move my lips against the glove. She lifted the train of her dress and quietly took my arm. In this silence, we mounted the staircase. I led her as if she were something holy. With parched lips, I finally asked:

"Would you care to dance?"

Narrowing her eyes, watching the rising heads in front of her, she slowly replied:

"I do not dance."

She passed into the ballroom, pausing near the doors. She continued to say nothing, as if I weren't there. But I could no longer control myself. Afraid I wouldn't have a more opportune moment, I burst forth with all I had rehearsed. I spoke with passion, with urgency, yet in a murmur. I assumed a casual expression so no one would notice this passion. And she, to my great joy, listened attentively—not interrupting me. As I spoke, she watched the dancers and steadily cooled herself with a fan made of smoke-colored ostrich feathers.

"I know," I said, not yet trusting my own words, "that I dare not have the slightest hope..." My face was composed, but my words were quick, ardent. Tormented, I restrained a quivering smile of happiness—I was so happy she was patiently listening to me, only pretending to be watching the dancers. "But you would not let me bring you here this evening..."

Not looking at me, she remarked in a tone of indifference:

"My coachman knows the way here quite well."

Thinking she was joking, I continued with greater insistence:

"Yes, I expect nothing in return. It is just enough for me to be standing here next to you, to have the wretched happiness of telling you at last, in full, what I have not dared say for so long... It is just this," I mumbled, wiping my icy forehead with a handkerchief, taking my eyes only briefly from her long, powdered eyelashes and her parted lips. "It is only this..."

Wriggling free of the dancers, a vivacious lady with chestnut hair came running up to us with a small woven basket which held a last bouquet of lilies of the valley. I glanced vacantly at the little face scattered with freckles and hastily dropped fifty rubles into the basket without taking the bouquet. The lady smiled sweetly, curtsied, and ran on. I wanted to continue where I'd left off, but couldn't—she had at last begun to speak:

"I'm fed up with that porcelain fool. You can't go to a single ball without running into her," she said, continuing to fan warm air onto me and watching a blonde gliding toward us with a Georgian officer. "It's a pity you didn't take the lilies. I would have kept them as a memento of this ball... However, it will still be memorable for me."

With difficulty, I deliriously paused to get my breath. Lowering my eyes, I asked:

"Memorable?"

She barely nodded in my direction:

"Yes. This isn't the first time I've listened to you say you love me. But now you have had, in your own words, the 'wretched happiness' of speaking 'in full' of your feelings. And so this ball shall also be memorable for me because I've already come to despise 'in full' both you and your ecstatic love. It might seem that nothing could be more touching, more beautiful than such a love! But what could be more intolerable, more insufferable, than when the woman herself is not in love? From this evening on, I don't think I'll have the strength to even see you near me. You suspect that I'm in love with someone else and for this reason am 'cold and pitiless.' Yes, I am in love. And do you know with whom? With my husband, whom you despise so much! Just think! He's more than twice my age. Up till now, he's been the biggest drunkard in the regiment. He's always red all over from being drunk. He's as uncouth as a sergeant, spends his days and nights with a certain Hungarian woman. I wouldn't be surprised if you do too! I'm in love!"

Stunned, I bowed to her and slowly picked my way through the crowd to the landing of the staircase. Suicide was my only resort after being so disgraced. But over there, in the crowd, stood an older gentleman. I had to walk around him on my way out. He was standing still, his legs apart, clasping an opera hat behind his back. Strong, crude-looking, he wore a baggy, threadbare frock coat. His hair was done *à la muzhik*. At that very moment, a tall, thin girl in a sheer, pale pink dress passed him carrying an open pearl fan, which she was gently shaking. Dead-drunk, covering her face with the fan, she slurred to him, "Tomorrow at four." And turning scarlet, she disappeared into the crowd. Still standing firmly with his legs apart, waving the opera hat a few times behind his back, the man closed his eyes and smiled with satisfaction—he'd heard her. I swaggered up to him boldly, like a real thug, and said:

"My dear sir, I dislike you intensely!"

He raised his eyebrows in amazement:

"What's with you? And with whom do I have the honor . . . "

I heatedly interrupted him:

"I will tell you who I am, then tell you what a boor you are, and challenge you to a duel!"

He snapped his legs together and straightened up.

"Are you drunk or just crazy?"

People were already gathering around us. I threw my calling card in his face and—gasping for air—stalked down the staircase in the triumphal, theatrical manner of a madman . . .

Of course, he never challenged me to a duel.

[1944]

Along a Familiar Street

LATE ONE NIGHT IN PARIS, I was walking along a boulevard in the thick, fresh, green semi-darkness that lay beneath street lights glittering like metal. I was relaxed, felt young, and thought:

> Along a familiar street
> An old house I recall
> A steep, dark staircase I would meet
> A curtained window tall . . .

What a marvelous verse! And how amazing that it all was once even mine! Moscow. The Presnya. The muffled sound of snow-covered streets. A shopkeeper's small, wooden house. And I, a student. It's hard to believe now that I was once that student . . .

> There a light full of mystery
> Would until midnight burn . . .

And it burned. And the snowstorm whirled, and the wind blew snow off the wooden roof, blowing it together with the chimney smoke. And a light was shining above, on the mezzanine, behind a red, cotton curtain . . .

> Ah, what a wondrous girl would then,
> That secret morning hour,
> Meet me in this old house again,
> That girl with flowing hair . . .

And that's just the way it was. The daughter of some church sexton in Serpukhov, a girl who had left her poverty-striken family and come to Moscow to continue her studies. And so I would walk up onto the small wooden porch covered with snow and pull the ring of the crackling doorbell wire leading into the front hallway. There the bell would tinkle with a tinny sound. The noise of feet running rapidly down steep wooden stairs would come from behind the door. The door would open. And the wind, the swirling snow would be carried into the house onto her, onto her shawl, her white blouse . . .

I'd lean down to kiss her, put my arms around her to shield her from the wind. And we'd race upstairs in the frosty cold, in the staircase darkness, run into her little room, which was also cold and dull in the light of a small kerosene lamp. The red curtain pulled in front of the window. Beneath it, the kerosene lamp sitting on a little table. And an iron bed next to a wall . . .

I'd throw of off my overcoat and cap, letting them fall where they might. Sitting on the bed, I'd draw her to me, seat her on my lap, feel her body—her small bones through her short skirt. Her hair would not be down around her shoulders, but up in large braids. The hair was a mousy brown. She had a common face, limpid from malnutrition. Her eyes were also limpid—peasant eyes. And her lips were tender like those of girls with no strength . . .

> Not with the ardor of a child
> Her lips would cling to mine,
> And trembling, with a whisper wild
> Say, "Listen! We must run!"

155

"Let's run away!" Where, why, from whom? This passionate, childish foolishness was so charming: "Let's run away!" We didn't do any "running away." There were those weak lips, the sweetest in the world. The hot tears that came to her eyes with the feeling of too much happiness, that intense anguish of young bodies that caused us to lean our heads on each other's shoulder. Her lips had grown hot, as if on fire, when I unbuttoned her blouse and kissed the young, milk-white breast with that strawberry-colored embryonic tip grown firm . . .

Coming to, she'd jump out of bed, light a spirit lamp, and warm up some thick tea. We'd wash down white bread and cheese wrapped in red paper. We'd talk endlessly of our future as we felt the winter, the fresh coldness drifting in from under the curtain, as we listened to the snow scattering against the windowpane.

"Along a familiar street an old house I recall . . . " What else do I recall? I recall that in the spring I went to see her off at the Kursk Station, that we rushed along the platform with her willow basket and the red blanket strapped into a bundle. I recall that we ran beside the long train preparing to leave, that we looked at the green cars packed with passengers. I recall how she finally clambered up into one of those narrow doorways, how I promised her I would come to Serpukhov in two weeks . . .

I recall no more, because there was no more.

[1944]

The Raven

MY FATHER LOOKED LIKE A RAVEN.
I got that impression when I was still a boy—I'd once seen a picture in *Niva* of Napoleon standing on some kind of cliff. He had a white paunch, was wearing suede pants and short, little black boots. And suddenly I roared with laughter remembering the pictures in Bogdanov's *Polar Travels*—I thought Napoleon looked so much like a penguin. And then I thought sadly: "But Papa looks like a raven . . . "

My father occupied a very prominent government post in our province town. And this ruined him all the more. I think that even in his own society of bureaucrats there was no one more difficult, sullen, curt, and coldly cruel. He was sluggish in his speech and behavior. Short, stocky, slightly stooped, with a crude kind of black hair, a long, dark, unshaven face, a large nose, he was the spitting image of a raven, especially when he was wearing black tails at the charity balls hosted by the Governor's wife. With stooped shoulders, he'd stand firmly rooted near some kind of kiosk shaped like a little Russian *izba*. He'd move his large raven's head and with shining eyes cast sidelong glances at the dancers, at the guests approaching the kiosk, even at that boyar's wife who, with a bewitching smile, would be taking squatty wine glasses of cheap yellow champagne out of the kiosk and giving them to guests with her large, diamond-studded hand. A brawny lady, she'd be wearing brocade and the headdress of a Russian peasant woman. Her nose would be powdered so pinkish-white that it seemed artificial.

My father had been a widower for a long time. He had only two children—my little sister Lilya and me. Our spacious, second-story government apartment sparkled coldly, emptily with its enormous mirror-clean rooms. It was located in a government apartment house with facades overlooking the boulevard lined with poplars. The boulevard ran between the cathedral and main street. Fortunately, I had been living for more than a year in Moscow, was studying there at the Katkovsky Lyceum, and came home periodically for Christmas and summer vacations. Yet that year, I was greeted by something totally unexpected.

I had graduated from the Lyceum in the spring. Having arrived from Moscow, I was simply staggered—it was as if the sun had suddenly appeared in our apartment, which up until then had been so funereal. All of it shone in the presence of this young, buoyant woman who had just replaced the nanny of my eight-year-old sister. That nanny had been a tall, tame old woman looking like a medieval wooden statue of some saint. This new nanny—a young woman with little money, the daughter of one of my father's low-level subordinates—was infinitely happy that she had found such a good job right after graduating from her Gymnasium. And at the time, she was glad that I—someone her own age—had arrived. But she was so afraid of my father that she quailed before him. During official dinners, she'd keep a vigilant, anxious eye on the dark-eyed Lilya, who was also curt and abrupt, not only in motion but also in repose, as if she were patiently waiting for something, yet all the while seeking it by turning her little black head!

My father became unrecognizable at dinners. He didn't look with the usual severity at Gury, the old man in cro-

cheted gloves who waited on him. He talked continuously—
slowly. Of course, he was paying attention only to her,
formally addressing her by her first name and patronymic—
"my dear Yelena Nikolayevna." He even tried to joke, to
laugh. But she was so embarrassed that she could answer
only with a pitiful smile—her tender face became splotched
with a faint scarlet. It was the face of a young, lean blonde
wearing a thin white blouse with underarms darkened by
hot, youthful perspiration. Small breasts were barely visible
beneath the blouse. At dinner, she never dared even to look
up at me. Here, I frightened her even more than my father
did. Yet the more she tried not to look, the colder my father
treated me. Both he and I sensed that a completely different
fear was concealed behind her tormented efforts to avoid
looking at me, to listen instead to what my father was
saying while she kept an eye on the malevolent, restless, yet
silent Lilya. That fear was the happiness she and I felt in
being so near to each other.

In the evenings, my father had always had his tea while
working at his desk. Even before he got there, the maid
would bring the large teapot, with its gilded edges into the
study and set it on his desk. But now, after the arrival of the
new nanny, he would have his tea in the dining room with
us. She'd sit on the other side of the samovar. By then, Lilya
would already be asleep. My father would come out of his
study wearing a long, wide, double-breasted jacket lined in
red. He'd sit in his armchair and hold out his cup to her.
She'd fill it to the brim—as he preferred—give it to him with
a trembling hand, pour some for herself and for me, and
with lowered eyelashes do some kind of needlework. He'd
talk slowly, in a strange way:

"My dear, blonde Yelena Nikolayevna. Does black or
crimson suit her? A dress that would go so well with your
face would be one of black satin with a jagged, stand-up
collar à la Mary Stuart, studded with small diamonds . . . Or
a medieval dress of crimson velvet, slightly décolleté, with a

little ruby cross... A little dark-blue coat of Lyons velvet and a Venetian beret would also suit you... Of course, these are just dreams," he'd say with a laugh. "Your father only gets seventy rubles a month from us. And besides you, he has five other children—his salary shrinks fast. That means that before you know it you're going to have to spend the rest of your life in poverty. But tell me all the same: What harm is there in dreaming? Dreams revive people, give them strength, hope. And then some dreams really do come true, don't they? Seldom, to be sure, but it does happen... After all, look at that cook who won a lottery not long ago at the railway station in Kursk—two hundred thousand rubles. And just an ordinary cook!"

She tried to give the impression of taking these remarks simply as pleasant jokes. She forced herself to look at him and smile. Pretending not to be listening, I played, "Napoleon," dealing the cards onto the table. One time, he went even further. Suddenly growing silent, he nodded in my direction:

"Most likely, this young man here also dreams. As they say, 'His papa will die sometime and his hens won't be pecking gold!' But those hens really will not be pecking, because there will be nothing to peck. Papa has, to be sure, a few things, such as a thousand *dessyatinas* of *chernozem* soil in Samara province. Only sonny will scarcely get his hands on them. He does not bestow much love on his papa and, as far as I can see, will turn out to be a number-one spendthrift."

This last conversation took place on the eve of Peter's Day—I remember it quite well. The next morning, my father drove off to the cathedral and, from there, to a name-day luncheon at the Governor's residence. Besides, he never had lunch at home on workdays. And so on this day, she and I had lunch together. Near the end of the meal, Lilya screamed at Gury in piercing shrieks when she was served a cherry pudding instead of her favorite pastry straws. Banging her little fists on the table, she hurled the plate onto the floor, started shaking her head, and choked with spiteful sobs. We somehow dragged her into her room—she was kicking, biting our arms. We got her calmed down by promising to punish the cook cruelly. She finally grew quiet and fell asleep. Both Yelena Nikolayevna and I experienced an acute feeling of anxious tenderness just in this—continually touching each other's hands while dragging Lilya to her room. Rain was sounding in the courtyard, lightning flashed fitfully in rooms growing dark, and windowpanes trembled from the thunder.

"The storm's having an effect on her," she whispered joyfully to me as we crept into the hallway. And she halted, listening carefully.

"Oh, there's a fire somewhere!"

We ran through the dining room, threw open a window, and saw a cart full of firemen rumbling past us down the boulevard. A downpour drenched the poplars. The storm had already passed—as if the rain had extinguished it. The fireman's bugle sounded playfully in a devilish way, sounded tenderly, warningly amid the rumbling of long carts being carried along, carts loaded with firemen wearing copper helmets, with their hoses and ladders amid the clamor of little bells on the manes of the black horses, amid the clatter of racing hooves as the carts galloped along the cobblestone street. Then the fire alarm sounded over and over again in the Bell Tower of Ivan the Charging Warrior.

We were side by side, close to each other, standing by the window which let in the fresh smell of water and the town's damp dust. And we seemed to be looking, listening with only intent excitement. Then we caught a glimpse of the last carts, with enormous red tanks on top. My heart beat faster, my forehead contracted—I took hold of her hand, hanging lifelessly at her side, and stared imploringly at her cheek. And she turned pale, opened her lips slightly, raised her breast with a sigh, and—as if also pleading—turned to me with bright, tear-filled eyes. I put an arm around her shoulder, and for the first time in my life found exquisite joy in the tender coldness of virginal lips . . .

After that moment, not a single day passed without the two of us meeting every hour. They seemed to be accidental encounters, whether in the living room, parlor, hallway, or even in the study—my father went there only in the early evening. Not a single day went by without those brief encounters, those kisses—desperately prolonged, insatiable, already unbearably tabooed. And my father, sensing something, again began drinking tea by himself in the study. He again became curt and sullen. But we no longer paid him any attention. And she grew more relaxed, more serious at dinner.

In early July, Lilya became ill from eating too many raspberries. She lay in her room and gradually improved. The whole time, she drew with crayons on large sheets of paper pinned to a board. She sketched fairy-tale cities, and Yelena Nikolayevna unwillingly stayed with her. Not leaving Lilya's bedside, she sat and knitted herself a small Little Russian shirt. There was no way she could leave—Lilya demanded something every minute. And I was perishing in the empty, silent house, perishing from the incessant, tormenting desire to see her, kiss her, hold her in my arms. I'd sit in my father's study, take whatever I came across in his bookcases, and try to read. I was sitting like that early one evening. I suddenly heard her light, rapid footsteps, threw the book aside and jumped up.

"What happened? Did she fall asleep?"

"Oh, no! You don't know, I guess. For two days straight, she hasn't been able to sleep. Nothing suits her. That's just the way it is with all lunatics! She sent me to look for some of her father's yellow and orange crayons."

And breaking into tears, she came to me and rested her head on my chest. I said:

"My God, when will all of this end! Why don't you just

come out and tell him that you love me, that nothing in the whole world can keep us apart!"

And looking up at me with a face wet with tears, she embraced me violently and gasped in a kiss. I pressed her whole body to me pulling her toward the divan. Was I really using my head? Did I remember anything? From the doorway of the study came a faint cough. I peered over her shoulder. My father was standing there—looking at us. Then he turned, slumped, and walked away.

None of us went to dinner. In the evening, Gury knocked at my door and announced: "Your papa wishes to see you." I walked into the study. He was sitting in the armchair facing the front of the desk. Not turning around, he began to talk:

"Tomorrow, you will be going away for the entire summer to my place in Samara province. In the autumn, you will have to make your own way to Moscow or Petersburg and find work there. If you dare disobey me, I will forever disinherit you. Moreover, tomorrow I will without delay ask the Governor to have you immediately sent to Samara province under police escort. Now go—and never show yourself to me again.

"Tomorrow, you will receive money for the trip and pocket expenses through an intermediary. By autumn, I will write my office in the village requesting that it give you a certain sum to start out with in the capitals. Have no hopes at all of seeing her before you leave. That is all, dear boy. Go."

That same night, I left for Yaroslav province, for the village where one of my close friends from the Lyceum lived. I stayed with him until autumn. At that time, through the influence of his father, I went to Petersburg and secured a position in the Ministry of Foreign Affairs. I wrote a letter to my father, telling him that I renounced not only my inheritance, but also any aid whatsoever from him. In the winter, I learned that he had retired and also moved to

Petersburg—"with a charming young wife," I was told.

One evening, I was walking down to the front rows of the Mariinsky Theater several minutes before the curtain went up. Suddenly, I saw both of them. They were sitting in a box near the stage, next to the railing—a small pair of mother-of-pearl opera glasses lay on it. He was in tails, stooped—like a raven—and reading attentively, squinting one eye at the program. She was moving with ease and grace. Her blonde hair was combed up. She gazed with animation all around—at the warm floor sparkling from the light of chandeliers, the floor being hidden by more and more arrivals making soft sounds. She gazed at the evening gowns, frock coats, and dress-uniforms of people entering the boxes.

A small ruby cross sparkled with a dark glow on her neck. Her slender, yet rounder, arms were bare. The flowing robe of a Roman goddess, a robe of crimson velvet, was pinned at her left shoulder with a ruby clasp . . .

[1944]

A Cold Autumn

IN JUNE OF THAT YEAR, he came to visit us at the estate. He had always felt at home there—his deceased father had been a friend and neighbor of my father. On June 15th, Ferdinand was killed in Sarajevo. On the morning of the sixteenth, they brought the newspapers from the post office. Holding a Moscow evening paper, my father rushed from the study into the dining room—where our guest, Mama, and I were still sitting at the table drinking tea—and said:

"Well, friends, it's war! The Austrian crown prince has been killed in Sarajevo. It's war!" On St. Peter's Day, my father's name-day, many people gathered at our house. At dinner, he announced my engagement to our guest. But on July 19th, Germany declared war on Russia.

In September, he came to stay with us for only a day to say farewell before leaving for the Front. (At the time, everyone thought the war would soon be over, and our wedding was postponed until spring.) And so our farewell evening arrived. After dinner, the maid brought the samovar in as she usually did. Looking at the windows misted over by its steam, my father said:

"The autumn is unusually early, unusually cold!"

We sat quietly that evening, only now and then exchanging insignificant words that were peaceful in an exaggerated sort of way. We concealed our innermost thoughts and feelings. With feigned simplicity, my father spoke once again of the autumn. I walked to the balcony door and wiped the windowpane with a shawl. Stars, clear and icy, were twinkling in the garden, in the black sky. My father was smoking, leaning back in his armchair as he gazed absentmindedly at the hot lamp hanging above the table. Wearing spectacles, Mama was sitting under its light diligently embroidering a small silk bag—we all knew for whom. The whole scene was emotional and uneasy. My father asked:

"So you still want to leave early in the morning, and not after lunch?"

"Yes, if that's all right—in the morning," he replied. "It's a very sad thing, but I still don't know now what to do with myself around the house."

My father sighed gently:

"Well, as you like it, dear boy. Only on this occasion, Mama and I must get some sleep. We don't want to miss seeing you off tomorrow ... "

Mama got up and made the sign of the cross over her future son-in-law. He bowed low to her hand, then to my father's. Now alone, both of us remained a little longer in the dining room. I thought of playing solitaire. He quietly paced from corner to corner, then asked:

"Would you like to take a short walk?"

My thoughts became even more oppressive. I answered indifferently:

"All right ... "

Putting on his coat in the front hallway, he seemed pensive. With a sweet smile, he recalled the lines of Fet:

Oh my, what a cold autumn I see!
I put on my housecoat and shawl ...

166

"I don't have a housecoat," I said. "But how does the rest of it go?"

> Look—between each blackening pine tree
> A fire seems to be rising tall . . .

"What fire?"

"The moon's coming up, of course. There's the special charm of a country autumn in these lines: 'I put on my housecoat and shawl . . . ' The times of our grandfathers and grandmothers . . . Oh, my God, my God!"

"What's the matter?"

"Nothing, sweetheart. I'm just sad. Sad, but all right. I love you very, very much . . . "

We put on our coats, crossed the dining room onto the balcony and went down to the garden. At first, it was so dark there that I held on to his sleeve. Gradually, we could see black twigs in the twinkling sky, twigs with the mineral sparkle of shining stars. Stopping suddenly, he turned around and looked at the house:

"Just see how the windows shine in a unique, autumn way. As long as I live, I shall forever remember this evening . . . "

I looked at the house, and he embraced me in my Swiss cloak. I drew the downy shawl from my face and tilted my head back so he could kiss me. While kissing me, he gazed into my face.

"How your eyes are shining," he said. "Aren't you cold? The air's just like winter. If I'm killed, you won't forget me right away, will you?"

I thought about it. Will he suddenly be killed? Could I really forget him so soon? Could I eventually forget everything? And I quickly answered, frightened by my own doubts:

"Don't talk that way! I couldn't bear your death!"

He grew silent, then said slowly, distinctly, "But if I am

killed, I shall wait for you there. Live life to the fullest, be happy—then come to me."

I began to weep bitterly . . .

He went away in the morning. Mama placed that fateful little bag around his neck, the one she had embroided the previous evening. In it was a golden icon, the one her father and grandfather had worn when they too had gone to war. And we made the sign of the cross over him in a kind of fitful despair.

Watching him leave, we stood on the porch with the stupefied feeling you always have whenever you say goodbye to someone you will not see for a long time. We felt only the astonishing contrast between us and the joyful, sunny, sparkling, frozen dew surrounding us that morning. We stood there a while, then returned to the empty house. I walked through the rooms with my hands behind my back, not knowing what to do with myself now, whether to start crying or singing at the top of my lungs . . .

He was killed—how strange it sounds!—the following month in Galicia. A full thirty years have passed since then. And I've endured many, so many things. The years seem long when you think about them, when you reflect on them, when you turn over in your mind that enchanted, inscrutable thing we call the past, something which neither our hearts nor our minds can comprehend.

In the spring of 1918, after my father and mother had died, I was living in Moscow in the Smolensk Market, in the basement belonging to a woman vendor. She was always making fun of me, saying, "Well, Your Excellency, how are things?" I too became a vendor. Like so many at the time, I sold to soldiers who were wearing Caucasian fur caps and unbuttoned greatcoats. I sold whatever I had left. A small ring. A little cross. A moth-eaten fur collar. And one day here, while selling at the corner of the Arbat and Market, I met a man who had an exceptional, beautiful soul. He was a middle-aged, retired soldier whom I soon married.

In April, we went to Yekaterinodar. We went there with his nephew, a boy of about seventeen, who was also trying to get through to the Volunteers. It took us almost two weeks. I traveled dressed as an old woman, wearing bast shoes. My husband wore a frayed, homespun Cossack coat. He'd grown a beard streaked with gray. For more than two years, we lived on the Don and Kuban. In the winter, in a hurricane, we joined masses of refugees taking passage on a ship sailing from Novorossiisk to Turkey. My husband died of typhus while we were at sea.

After that, I had only three people in the whole world— my husband's nephew, his young wife, and their little girl, who was seven months old. But after a while, the nephew and his wife took a ship to the Crimea, to Wrangel. They left the child with me. And they disappeared without a trace.

For a long time, I lived in Constantinople, earning a living for myself and the little girl by taking on hard, menial work. Then, like so many others, the two of us wandered all over! Bulgaria, Serbia, Bohemia, Paris, Nice . . . The little girl grew up long ago, remained in Paris, and became French in every way. She was very nice, totally unconcerned about me. She worked in a chocolate store near the Madelaine. Her well-groomed hands with their silver fingernails wrapped boxes in gigantic pieces of paper and tied them with little golden strips of lace. But I lived in Nice and for that matter still live there, getting by with the grace of God . . . I first visited Nice in 1912. If during those happy days I'd only known what that city would one day mean to me!

And so I did live through his death, though I had once said I couldn't bear it. Yet in thinking back on everything I have gone through since then, I always ask myself, "Well, was there anything special in your life?" And I reply, "Only that cold, autumn evening."

Did it really exist? It really did. And everything else in my life has been what was left over—a useless dream. And I believe, yes, I fervently believe, that somewhere he is waiting for me, waiting with the same love and youthfulness of that evening.

"Live life to the fullest, be happy—then come to me." I have lived life to the fullest. I've been happy. And soon, now, I shall come.

[1944]

Three Rubles

T HAT SUMMER EVENING,
I had taken the train from my country estate and arrived at
about nine in our district town. It was still hot—a thunder-
storm was gloomily moving in with the rain clouds. As a
horse-drawn cab rushed past me—kicking up dust from the
railway station along the darkening fields—something
behind me suddenly blazed. The road ahead flashed gold.
Thunder rolled in the distance and a quick, scattered rain
came down like big stars, spanking the dust and cab—and
abruptly stopping. The cab broke free of the ground
beneath the soft surface of a long, gradual slope, then began
rattling over a stone bridge that crossed the dried-up bed of a
stream. On the other side of the bridge, the town's forges
were a savage black, smelling of metal. A dusty kerosene
lamp sat at the side of the road where the cab began to
ascend the mountain.

In the Vorobeva Hotel—the best in town—the bellboy
took me as usual to a room which had a bed behind a
partition. The oven-hot air in this room came in through
two open windows hidden behind white calico curtains. I
had the bellboy open the windows all the way, then bring in

a samovar. I walked quickly to the window—you couldn't even breathe in the room.

The darkness outside the window deepened to black. The lightning flared sporadically—now it was blue—and the thunder rumbled as if it were rolling over potholes. I remember musing for a long time. I didn't understand why this insignificant, backwater town even existed, or why this magnificent blue light was blazing so threateningly above it, why it was roaring so majestically, shaking the somber, invisible sky.

I went behind the partition. While taking off my coat and undoing my tie, I heard the bellboy race in with a samovar on a tray and tap it down onto the round table in front of the divan. I peered around the partition—besides the samovar, a finger bowl, a glass, and a roll on a plate, there was a single cup on the tray.

"Why the cup?" I asked.

With an all-knowing look, the bellboy replied:

"A lady is asking for you, Boris Petrovich."

"What kind of lady?"

The bellboy shrugged and answered with a fake smile:

"The usual kind. She really begged me to let her in, promised to pay me a ruble for the tea if she makes good money. She saw you drive up . . . "

"Is she a streetwalker?"

"That's pretty obvious. But we've never had them as plain. Guests usually send to Anna Matveyevna for ladies, and right off one of them shows up . . . She's remarkably tall. Looks like a Gymnasium student."

I thought a while about the boring evening which lay ahead, then said:

"It sounds like fun. Let her in."

The bellboy joyfully disappeared. I began boiling water for the tea, but right away there was a knock at the door. I looked up in amazement—without waiting for me to answer, a tall young woman with large feet casually walked in. She wore old linen slippers, a brown Gymnasium dress, and a little straw hat with a bunch of small, artificial cornflowers at one side.

"I saw the light in your window and decided to drop by," she said, trying to smile ironically, her dark eyes to one side.

I hadn't expected any of this. I was a little astonished and answered with exaggerated gaiety:

"I'm very glad to meet you. Take your hat off and have some tea."

Behind the curtains, the sky was flashing now with broad strokes of violet light. The thunder rolled threateningly somewhere nearby. The scent of wind blew into the room, and I rushed to close the window, happy to have a chance to hide my embarrassment. When I turned around, she was sitting on the divan, having taken off her hat and now pushing back her short hair with an oblong, suntanned hand. Her hair was thick and chestnut-colored. She had broad cheekbones, freckles, full lips the color of lilacs, and dark, serious eyes. I wanted to excuse myself in a joking way for not wearing a coat, but she looked at me coldly and asked:

"How much will you pay?"

Again I replied, trying to seem carefree:

"We've still got time to decide that! Let's drink some tea first."

"No," she said with a frown, "I must know the conditions first. I won't take less than three rubles."

"Then three rubles it is," I said in that same stupid, irresponsible manner.

"Are you joking?" she asked harshly.

"Not at all," I answered, thinking I would fill her with tea, give her three rubles, and wish her well.

She sighed, shut her eyes, and leaned her head back against the divan. I thought for some time as I looked at her bloodless, lilac lips. I thought that most likely she was hungry. I gave her the plate with the roll, sat next to her on the divan, and touched her hand:

"Please have something to eat."

She opened her eyes and started quietly eating and drinking. I stared at her suntanned hands and the dark eyelashes austerely lowered. I thought that this affair was going to take an even more ridiculous turn, and asked:

"Are you from around here?"

She gently shook her head, washed down the roll, and replied:

"No, from far away . . ."

And she again grew silent. Then she brushed the crumbs off her lap and suddenly stood up, not looking at me:

"I'm going to get undressed."

This was most unexpected. I wanted to say something, but she imperiously interrupted me:

"Lock the door and shut the blinds."

And she disappeared behind the partition.

Hastily, with an unconscious submissiveness, I shut the blinds. As if trying to peer even deeper into the room, the lightning continued flashing even brighter from behind them. And the thunder rumbled all the more persistently. I turned the key in the lock, not understanding why I was doing all this. I would have liked to go to her, laugh insincerely, turn everything into a joke, or lie to her, saying I had a terrible headache. But she loudly said from behind the partition:

"Come . . ."

And again I unconsciously obeyed her, went behind the partition and saw her already lying in bed. She lay there with the blanket pulled up to her chin, looking wildly at me with eyes that had become totally black, tightly pursing her lips, which she gently tapped from time to time against the blanket. And in the forgetfulness of passion, I jerked the blanket from her hands and uncovered her entire body, clothed only in a short, soiled slip. She was barely able to grab the wooden ball hanging above the head of the bed, and put out the light . . .

I stood in the darkness near the open window, greedily smoked a cigarette, listened to the sound of a downpour falling in a sheet as it rushed about in the black darkness lying above the dead town, rushed with the clear, rapid quiverings of violet lightning and distant claps of thunder. I inhaled the rainy freshness mingling with the smells of the town, heated up by the sun during the day. And I said to myself, "Yes, an inexplicable union. This wretched, godforsaken place and this majesty—threatening, thundering, blinding as if divine." I marveled even more and was horrified by the thought—"How was it that I did not as yet fully understand the woman I would be making love to? And why had she decided to sell her virginity—yes, her virginity!—for three rubles?" She called to me:

"Close the window—it's too noisy—and come here."

In the darkness, I returned behind the partition, sat on the bed, found her hand, and as I kissed it said:

"Forgive me, forgive me . . . "

She asked impassively:

"You thought I was a real prostitute, didn't you? And a very stupid or crazy one at that, right?"

I hastily replied:

"No, no, not crazy. I only thought that you were still young, inexperienced, though you already know that some of the girls in the best-known houses wear the Gymnasium dress."

"Why?"

"To seem more innocent, more attractive."

"No, I didn't know that. I just don't have any other dress. I just graduated from school this past spring. And Papa died right away—Mama died a long time ago. I came from Novocherkassk thinking I'd find a job here through a relative. I stayed at his place, he started coming on to me, I hit him, and since then have been sleeping at night on park benches . . . I thought I'd die when I came into this room. But then I saw that you wanted somehow to get rid of me."

175

"Yes, I got myself into a stupid situation," I said. "I agreed to let you come in simply because I was bored—I've never had anything to do with prostitutes. I thought that the most ordinary streetwalker would come walking in, I'd treat her to tea, gab a little, joke a little, and then would simply give her two or three rubles."

"Yes, and I showed up instead. Up until the last minute, I tried to keep telling myself only one thing—'three rubles, three rubles.' But something happened which I didn't at all expect. Now I don't understand anything."

Even I didn't understand anything—the darkness, the sound of the downpour outside the windows, some Gymnasium girl from Novocherkassk lying near me on the bed, a girl whose name I didn't even know. And then these feelings I had for her, feelings which grew uncontrollable with each passing minute . . . I said with difficulty:

"What don't you understand?"

She didn't answer. I suddenly turned the light on. Her large, black eyes, full of tears, flashed before me. She impetuously sat up and—biting her lip—rested her head on my shoulder. I tilted it back, began kissing her distorted mouth wet with tears, and embraced her large body clad in the soiled slip which by now was hanging from one shoulder. Delirious with feelings of pity and tenderness, I saw her girl's feet darkened by dust . . .

The hotel room was full of the morning sun coming in through the lowered blinds. Yet we were still sitting on the divan talking in front of the round table. Still famished, she drank down the cold tea left over from the night before and ate the rest of the roll. And all the while we kissed each other's hands.

She stayed at the hotel, I made a short trip to the country, and the next day both of us left for Mineralnye Vody.

We wanted to spend the autumn in Moscow, yet spent both the autumn and winter in Yalta. Her temperature started going up and she began coughing. Our rooms smelled of creosote . . . And in the spring I buried her.

A Yalta cemetery high on a hill. From here, you can see the faraway sea. From the city—crosses and monuments. And among them, probably even now, a marble cross yet shines with a pristine whiteness on one of the graves most dear to me. And now I will never see it again—God in His mercy has spared me this.

[1944]

The Swing

ONE SUMMER NIGHT, he was sitting in the living room banging on the piano keys. He heard her footsteps on the balcony, struck the keys wildly, and began singing out of tune, crying:

> I don't envy gods afar
> I don't envy any tsar,
> When I see your languishing stare,
> Slender waist and dark tresses fair!

She walked in wearing a blue sarafan with two long, dark braids down her back. She had on a coral necklace. The blue eyes of her suntanned face laughed when she asked:

"Is all of this about me? And an aria you composed yourself?"

"Yes!"

And he again struck the keys and cried out:

> I don't envy gods afar . . .

"My, what an ear for music you have!"

"I'm also a famous painter. And handsome like Leonid Andreyev. I'd rush to your rescue!"

" 'He scares some people, but he doesn't scare me.' That's what Tolstoy said about your Andreyev."

"We'll see, we'll see!"

"And my grandfather's crutch!"

"Even though your grandfather's a hero of Sevastopol, he only looks tough. We'll run away, get married, then throw ourselves at his feet—breaking into tears and begging his forgiveness . . . "

At twilight, before dinner, as the pungent odor of meat-balls and fried onions wafted from the kitchen and a dewy coldness descended on the park, they stood together on a swing at the end of a tree-lined path. They swung on it facing each other. The swing screeched and caused the hem of her dress to puff out as it moved. As he gripped the ropes in a backward stroke, his eyes became terrible. Turning red, she stared vacantly, joyfully.

"Hey! Over there's the first star and a new moon and the green, green sky above the sea. Mr. Painter, just look how thin the crescent is! The moon, the moon, its golden cres-cent . . . Oh, we're breaking loose!"

Flying down and jumping off onto the ground, they sat on the swing's wooden seat, trying to control their excited breathing while looking at each other.

"Well? I told you so!"

"Told me what?"

"You've already fallen in love with me."

"Perhaps. Get up. They're calling us for dinner. Hey, let's go, let's go!"

"Wait a minute. The first star, a new moon, a green sky, the smell of dew, the kitchen smells—again, probably my favorite dish, meatballs in sour cream!—and the blue eyes and beautiful, happy face . . . "

"Yes, it seems as if there will never be a happier evening in my life . . . "

"Dante said of Beatrice, 'Love began with her eyes and ended with her lips.' Is that so?" he asked, taking her hand.

She looked down, closed her eyes, and leaned her face toward him. He put his arms around her shoulders with their gentle braids, then lifted her chin:

"And ended with her lips?"

"Yes . . . "

He looked at the ground as they were walking down the lane:

"But what should we do now? Should we run to your grandfather, fall on our knees, and ask for his blessing? But what kind of husband would I make?"

"No, no, anything but that."

"But what then?"

"I don't know. Let's just go on like we are . . . It could not be better."

[1945]

Bernard

M Y DAYS REMAINING ON earth are now few. And so I recall what I once jotted down about Bernard when I was in the Coastal Alps, near Antibes.

"I was sound asleep when Bernard tossed a handful of sand at my window ... "

Thus begins Maupassant's *On the Water.* That is how Bernard awakened him before the *Bel Ami* left the port of Antibes on April 6, 1888.

"I opened the window, and the smell of the enchanting night closeness struck me in the face, the chest, the heart. The clear blueness of the sky trembled with the lively brilliance of stars ...

" 'It's good weather, sir.'

" 'And the wind?'

" 'From the shore, sir.' "

A half an hour later, they were already at sea:

"The horizon grew pale, and in the distance, beyond Angels' Bay, we could see the lights of Nice. Even farther— the rotating beacon of Villefranche ... From the mountains, not yet visible, a dry, cold breath occasionally drifted toward the yacht. I could just feel that the mountains were covered with snow ...

"As soon as we left port, the yacht came alive. It became gay, sailed faster, danced on a small ripple . . . Day arrived, the stars went out . . . In the distant sky above Nice, the snowy ridges of the Higher Alps had already begun to burn with a certain glow . . .

"I gave the wheel to Bernard so I could admire the sunrise. A strong breeze was driving us along a quivering wave. I heard a faraway bell—the Angelus was sounding . . . How I love this easy, fresh morning hour, when people are still asleep and the earth is beginning to awake! You inhale, drink, see the physical life of the world being born—life, whose secret is our great, eternal torment . . .

"Bernard is thin, agile, conscientious, and vigilant, with an unusual devotion to cleanliness and order. He is a frank, loyal man, a superb sailor . . . "

That is how Maupassant spoke of Bernard. Yet Bernard said the following of himself:

"I think I was a good sailor. *Je crois bien que j'étais un bon marin.*"

He said this as he was dying—these were the last words he uttered on his deathbed in the same Antibes he had left on the *Bel Ami* on April 6, 1888.

A man who had seen Bernard not long before his death says:

"Over the span of many years, Bernard had shared the great poet's vagabond sea life, never leaving his side until Maupassant's fatal departure for Paris to see Doctor Blanche.

"Bernard died in his Antibes. But not long before, I had seen him on the sunny shoreline of the small port of Antibes, where the *Bel Ami* had so often been anchored.

"Tall, withered, with an energetic face hardened by saltwater, Bernard had never been very talkative. Yet if you even mentioned the name of Maupassant, how his blue eyes would light up with animation! You should have heard how he talked about him.

"He is now forever silent. His last words were, 'I think I have been a good sailor.' "

My lively imagination pictured just how he had said these words. I could see him saying them resolutely, proudly, crossing himself with a black hand shriveled with age:

"Je crois bien que j'étais un bon marin."

"But what had he meant by them? Was it the joy of realizing that while living on earth he had, as a good sailor, helped those around him? No, he meant that God gives everyone of us along with life itself some kind of talent. And He entrusts us with the sacred task of not letting it die. Why? For what purpose? We do not know. Yet we must know that everything in this world that we find so incomprehensible has meaning, an exalted, divine purpose intended to make everything on earth 'good.' And we must know that in fervently fulfilling this divine plan, we are serving Him. For this reason, we should do it with a sense of joyful pride.

"Bernard both knew and sensed this. Throughout his life, he had ardently fulfilled this humble duty in a commendable manner, this duty which God had entrusted to him and which Bernard had fulfilled not out of a sense of fear or guilt. How then could he not have said what he did at the final moment of his life? 'Unto you, Lord, I return Your servant, and can courageously tell You and all people, 'I think I have been a good sailor.' "

"Everything worried Bernard at sea," Maupassant wrote. "And suddenly he sailed into a current of air which spoke of a breeze blowing somewhere far above the open sea, of clouds above the Esterel—called the Mistral in the South . . . He kept the yacht so clean that he could not bear to see even a drop of water on any brass surface . . . "

But how could Bernard have really been of any use to anyone by immediately wiping off this drop of water? But he did it anyway. Why? For what purpose?

But God Himself really does love everything that is

"good." He Himself takes joy in all of His creations being "very good."

It seems to me that I, as an artist, have in my final days earned the right to say something similar to what Bernard, in dying, said.

[1952]

Notes

FROM THE AUTHOR

Excerpts from Bunin's introduction to *Vesnoi, v iudeye; Roza ierikhona* (New York: Izdatelstvo imeni Chekhova, 1953). Bunin died in Paris on November 8, 1953.

Karamzin: Nikolai Mikhailovich Karamzin (1766-1826). Russian writer and historian.

Strelets: A "musketeer." The *streltsy* were the Russian equivalent of the Praetorian Guard.

Tsarevna Sofia: Regent of Russia from 1682 to 1689. Peter the Great's older stepsister. She attempted to depose him and install herself as Empress in 1698. The *streltsy* participated in the aborted coup.

WOLVES

Gymnasium student: Gymnasiums were a special kind of secondary school in tsarist Russia. The boys' Gymnasiums were created in 1804, the girls' Gymnasiums in 1858.

Izba: The traditional Russian peasant cottage, somewhat resembling a log cabin.

"Little Russia": Until 1917, Russians commonly referred to the Ukraine as Little Russia.

Verst: Approximately two-thirds of a mile.

"Rows of old Jewish shops": The Russian word *ryad* has been translated as "shop." Actually, a *ryad* was a narrow, windowless wooden stall which served as a place of business. Its single door was locked after hours. For a brief description of a Jewish *ryad*, see Isaak Babel's short story *Gedali*.

IN AUGUST

"hooted": Again, Bunin emphasizes the significance of the town's Polish population by employing the verb *gukat,* which is a Russianized form of the Polish *hukác*—"to hoot."

"little masters": The word Bunin uses is *panychi,* the diminutive of *pan,* Polish for "master." By referring to these people as *panychi,* Bunin is stressing the ethnic importance of Poles in this Ukrainian town.

Podol: A Russian word designating the lower part of a mountain. In Russian towns situated on low-lying mountains, the poorer residents often lived and worked "on the *Podol.*" Many Jews living in this area adopted the surname "Podolsky."

"They arrested Pavlovsky": Tolstoy encouraged his followers to refuse military service. "If you think it unreasonable to kill the Turks or the Germans," he wrote in *What I Believe,* "then do not kill them."

Tolstoyans: Advocates of the religious views of the Russian writer Leo Tolstoy (1828-1910). Based on Christianity, Tolstoyanism stressed nonviolence, renunciation of property, and living the simple life. Especially ironic in the context of this story, Tolstoyanism also condemned marital infidelity and lust. In the late nineteenth century, many young Russians from wealthy families embraced Tolstoyanism and went "back to nature."

A NEW YEAR

Dessyatina: Approximately twenty-seven acres.

Stove-bench: A kind of bunk often built beside Russian stoves, particularly in peasant homes. Many peasants preferred to sleep on the stove-bench because it was one of the warmest places in the house.

"Tatyana in an open dress . . . ": Lines from Alexander Pushkin's *Eugene Onegin.* Some Russian women of the eighteenth century believed that by looking at the moon's reflection in a mirror they could guess the name of their future husband. In the context of this story, the verse is especially ironic. Tatyana fell in love with Onegin, who rejected her. Years later, he fell in love with her, but then she rejected him.

Traveler's-joy: A European climbing plant with greenish-white flowers.

GENTLE BREATHING

"expensive combs": A graduate of a girls' Gymnasium recalls, "Rings, brooches, bracelets, and beads were strictly forbidden. It was also forbidden to have one's hair curled." (Sophie Satina, *Education of Women in Pre-Revolutionary Russia,* trans. Alexandra F. Poustchine [New York: By the Author, 1966], p.51.)

Mukden: A city in Manchuria defended by a Russian army which was defeated by Japanese forces during the Russo-Japanese War. The battle lasted from February 19 to March 10, 1905.

Schoolgirl: The word *gimnazistka* has been translated as "schoolgirl," though it designates a female Gymnasium student. As already noted, the girls' Gymnasiums were special schools created for females in 1858. Their curricula were more modest than those of the boys' Gymnasiums, which emphasized study of the classics. Although many girls' Gymnasiums did not offer instruction in either Latin or Greek, they did provide coursework in French and German. Girls' Gymnasiums were originally designed for students from wealthy families. By the end of the nineteenth century, however, select students from lower-class families were being admitted.

Russian girls receiving Gymnasium educations normally began study at the age of nine or ten and graduated at sixteen or seventeen. Every girls' Gymnasium had a principal (headmistress) assisted by form mistresses, who were responsible for overseeing a single class of students through seven years in the school. All Gymnasium girls were required to wear uniforms—dark brown dresses with black aprons. Girls who completed seven years of Gymnasium study were qualified to teach in grammar schools. Those completing an optional eighth year ("the pedagogical class") could become private tutors and/or enroll in higher courses for women without taking any entrance examinations.

Many young women graduating from Gymnasiums did none of these, but became housewives.

THE PASSING

"old women": Professional mourners, common at Russian funerals.

Pilgrim: For centuries in tsarist Russia, male and female pilgrims wandered the country begging alms. Although many Westerners would regard most of these pilgrims to be emotionally-disturbed vagrants, Russians commonly viewed them as holy— "fools in Christ." Russians generally considered it a sin to refuse a pilgrim alms.

SUNSTROKE

Anapa: A resort town located on the northeastern shore of the Black Sea.

THE MORDVINIAN SARAFAN

"Mordvinian sarafan": Mordvinia is today the Mordvinian Autonomous Soviet Socialist Republic, located in the Middle-Volga Region (capital: Saransk). A sarafan is a full-length, sleeveless garment which Russian peasant women wore over a slip.

AN ENDLESS SUNSET

Drozhky: A small, open, Russian carriage. A bench ran down the center, and passengers either straddled it or sat sideways.

Jackdaw: A European crow.

Knout: A thick, hard leather whip approximately 3' long.

"Now we'll have sunset all night long": Reference is to the "white nights," that period of continual sunlight which occurs in the northern part of the USSR in late spring and during the summer.

THE MURDERESS

Mezzanine: In this context, a low-ceilinged partial story projecting like a balcony over the ground story.

Zamoskvorechya: An old section of Moscow located across the Moscow River from Red Square.

Arbat: An old section in central Moscow where many Russian artists of the nineteenth century lived.

"burial mounds": Barrows in which ancient Slavs buried their dead.

Gelendzhik, Gagra: Gelendzhik is a Black Sea resort located southeast of Novorossiisk. Gagra is also a Black Sea resort, located southeast of Sochi.

"making the sign of the cross over her": A custom in tsarist Russia when people were leaving on a journey.

Narzan: A kind of mineral water.

"The second bell rang": Trains in tsarist Russia departed at the sound of a third bell.

MUZA

"Muza Graf": The name is ironic in several respects. *Muza* means "muse." *Graf* is a title of nobility—a Count.

"small dachas had been built and were being rented out": In the late nineteenth and early twentieth century, some destitute Russian landowners resorted to this dacha rental plan to avoid being forced to sell their land. In Anton Chekhov's play *The Cherry Orchard*, Lopakhin advises Lyubov Andreyevna to build dachas on her estate and rent them so she would be able to retain possession of the land.

RUSYA

"Amata nobis quantum amabitur nulla!": "Loved by us as no other will be loved!"

Corncrake: A marsh bird brown on top and yellowish-white underneath. A popular game bird in Europe.

Kvass: A mildly intoxicating Russian drink made by fermenting bread in water.

Niva: A popular Russian illustrated magazine published from 1870 to 1918.

"No wonder the word 'horror' comes from 'grass snake.' ": The Russian word for "grass snake" is *uzh*, while that for "horror" is *uzhas*.

"when I was taking courses": For Russian women of the late nineteenth century, "taking courses" was roughly the equivalent of attending college.

ANTIGONE

"Alexander": Because the general was elderly, he most likely served under two Russian tsars named Alexander. The portrait was either of Alexander II (1818-1881) or Alexander III (1845-1894).

Averchenko: Arkady Timofeyevich Averchenko (1881-1925). Russian humorist who emigrated from his homeland after the Revolution.

Octave Mirbeau: French writer (1848-1917). Works marked by anarchism and anticlericalism.

Russo-Japanese War: Began on February 8, 1904, and ended on September 5, 1905.

A LITTLE FOOL

"begging alms": (See note in THE PASSING for "Pilgrim.") For a moving eyewitness account of convicts begging alms in tsarist Russia, see George Kennan's *Siberia and the Exile System* (Chicago: University of Chicago Press, 1958).

GALYA GANSKAYA

Galya: Shortened form of Galina.

"Garçon, un demi!": "Waiter, a half!"

"kissed the soft, aromatic beard": In Russia, there was and is no homosexual significance in men kissing each other as a form of greeting and farewell.

"Vieux satyr!": "Old satyr!"

THE VISITOR

Sunday School: Special schools for the poor created in Russia in the late 1850s. Supervised entirely by volunteers (including Tolstoy), these schools were primarily secular; they were called "Sunday" Schools because that was the one day of the week peasants had free time to attend them. The purpose of the schools was to raise the intellectual and moral level of the general populace. It is quite ironic that Adam Adamych is corrupting the morals of a cook while her mistress—his personal friend—is teaching at a Sunday School in a working-class section of St. Petersburg.

A MEMORABLE BALL

"à la muzhik": "In the style of a Russian peasant."

"come to Moscow to continue her studies": At the turn of the century, Russian women desiring financial independence, especially those seeking to improve their station in life, often enrolled in "higher courses" in St. Petersburg or Moscow after completing secondary school. Many of these *kursistki* became teachers, surgical assistants, or physicians.

Presnya: A section of Moscow located in the western part of the city.

THE RAVEN
"Bell Tower of Ivan the Charging Warrior": Probably named after Ivan III, Grand Duke of Muscovy and Vladimir (1440-1505). He was also known as Ivan the Great.

"Napoleon": A kind of solitaire.

Peter's Day: Russians of the period celebrated their birthdays not on the date of their birth, but rather on the date commemorating the Christian saint after whom they were named. This was their "name-day." Peter's Day (St. Peter's Day) was on June 29 (Old Style).

"the capitals": Russians of the period frequently referred to St. Petersburg (the capital at the time) and Moscow (the former capital) as the "capitals."

"That means that before you know it you're going to have to spend the rest of your life in poverty.": A particularly cruel remark. For many women in nineteenth-century Russia who were not from wealthy families, were unmarried, and earned their own livings as teachers or governesses, the prospect of poverty in old age was their greatest fear.

"under police escort": An incredibly extreme measure. The Raven is treating his son as if the young man were a criminal. On the way to Samara province, the police escort would have to stop at the *étapes* where convicts made periodic stops on their way to Siberian exile.

A COLD AUTUMN
"Ferdinand was killed in Sarajevo": Austrian Archduke Franz Ferdinand was assassinated in Sarajevo on June 28, 1914 (New Style).

Fet: Afanasy Afanasyevich Fet (1820-1892). Russian poet.

Volunteers: The anti-Bolshevik troops who fought in southern Russia during the Russian Civil War (1918-1921).

Wrangel: Baron Peter Nikolayevich Wrangel (1878-1928). Prominent anti-Bolshevik leader who commanded the Volunteers from December 1919 to January 1920.

Yekaterinodar: Pre-Revolutionary name of Krasnodar.

THREE RUBLES

Mineralnye Vody: A health resort in the Caucasus where Russians went for mineral baths.

"short hair": Gymnasium girls with short hair were nonconformists who often engaged in various kinds of anti-establishment activity.

THE SWING

Leonid Andreyev: Leonid Nikolayevich Andreyev (1871-1919). Popular Russian writer noted for his good looks. An ardent anti-Bolshevik, Andreyev emigrated from Russia after the Revolution

Sevastopol: Crimean city where Russian defenders withstood the eleven-month siege of armies from Great Britain, France, Turkey, and Sardinia during the Crimean War (1853-1856).